Out of Control

Sierra Denise

Street Fiction

Copyright © 2014 Sierra Seabrooks
All rights reserved.
ISBN-10: 0692297227
ISBN-13: 978-0692297223

This book is dedicated to my late father John Seabrooks Jr. I know you didn't think much of me writing, but I just wanted to say "Daddy I made it!"
I love you

RIP Daddy

(October 29, 1929 – February 19, 2014)

Also in remembrance of my late sister Pamela Cornelia Coleman. "I love you with all my heart and you are truly missed."

RIP Pam

(December 5, 1974 – June 15, 2013)

~   ~   ~

I woke up from my sleep like I did every morning at this time, awaiting the arrival of my dad from a long night of making sure his army of men was handling his business the right way.

My dad Sam 'Gunz' Smith was one of the biggest drug kingpins in the state. He moved major weight in our city. The smaller drug dealers hated that and hated him. Although my dad was a drug dealer, that didn't matter to me. He was a great father, husband and provider for his family.

It was just my mom, him and I, and we had anything we could have ever wanted. My dad had recently brought me a car that I loved.

My mom Faith Smith adored my dad. They had been together since high school and remained together since then. She was the sweetest person ever, but if you crossed her, she would make sure you'd never do it again. My dad would often say, "Sometimes Faith, you can be as cold as ice.", which he nicked named her. 'ICE'. She had it plated on the car that he had brought her.

It was like clockwork when my dad came home, so I went and sat in the window and watched as he got out of the car and started from cross the street. He looked up at me and smiled, which always warmed my heart, because I was a huge daddy's girl. Unlike most girls that I've grown up around, my dad had always been there, and we lived a very happy life, because he treated his two ladies like queens.

When my daddy was making his way across the street, I saw two guys dressed in all black come creep from the side of the street he parked on. When they got close behind him they pulled out their guns. I was so much in shock that I couldn't say a word to warn my dad. When he turned around and saw the guys behind him, I ran out of my room and started downstairs, but before I could make it halfway down, gunshots went off. I dropped down to the floor and covered my head praying that everything would be over and my dad would be ok.

After twelve shots there was silence until I heard my mom yell out in horror. I went down stairs and to the front door and saw my dad all shot up, breathing what would be his last few breaths. My mom was hysterically crying, in shock. Tears started pouring from my eyes, but yet I was still silent. I sat down and laid my dad's head in my lap and he started coughing up blood.

"Please Sam, please don't leave me. Don't die." My mom cried out. "Yolanda call 911."

I ran in the house and called 911 and explained what happened. "My dad's been shot, please send help. We live at 615 W35th and Grady. Please hurry." I hung up and ran back outside before the dispatcher could ask any more questions.

When I got back, he rolled his eyes up to me and he started coughing as he tried to speak. "Baby," he coughed again spitting blood. "I want you to always know... I love you and your mama." He coughed one last time, and his eyes closed.

"Daddy, wake up. Wake up daddy. Please don't leave us, you can't." I started yelling and screaming.

Sirens of the ambulance and police were heard coming down the street, and people started coming out of their homes to witness the aftermath of my father's murder.

The paramedics got out of the ambulance and came over.

"You're too late. Get away from him. Get away." She sounded delirious.

"Ma, please let them do their job."

She allowed me to help her up and she cried on my shoulder as we hugged. Paramedics tried to revive him, but he was clearly gone. They got out the gurney and put my dad's lifeless body on it. My mom got in the ambulance with them, but I just couldn't. It was hard to face the facts of what had just happened. I couldn't believe that my dad was gone.

Chapter 1

Even after eight years of my dad murder, I would frequently have daydreams and nightmares of the night he was killed. His death left a big dent in our family that could never be filled. My mom turned to drinking to rid her of her sorrows.

With her drinking, it caused a lot of friction in our mother-daughter relationship. We would often argue about things, be it small or big. I hated to see my mother this way, but she didn't see how her drinking was hurting me and herself.

Tonight we got into an argument, so I called my friend up so that we could go out. I couldn't stay in the house, because it irritated me to see her that way.

"NaNa are you ready, because if you not I'm leaving your ass right there."

"What, you leaving right now?" She asked.

"In a minute I'll be over there. Ma trippin, so I got to get up out here."

"I'll be ready when you get here."

"Ok. I'll hit you up when I get outside."

"Ok."

I hang up and continue to get ready.

If you're wondering, my name is Yolanda Smith, but all my friends call me Applez. I'm a about 5'5", I have a light brown complexion, and thick in all the right places. My hair was past my shoulders and it was a deep silky brown. I'm currently single and I have been since my boyfriend Ace was killed two years ago from a stray bullet when while he was at the court playing ball with his friends. I was in love with him and he was there for me when my dad died. After I lost him, I didn't date or want to talk to anyone else.

Don't get me wrong a lot of people tried to talk to me, but my mind wasn't even close to wanting be in a relationship. I was trying to focus on myself.

Before I left out of my room, I had to check myself out in the mirror. "Damn I look good." I had on a nice little navy blue bodycon dress, with some black pumps on.

When I left the house my mama wasn't home. She probably was gone to her so called friend Stacie house. She was her drinking partner.

I got into my car that my dad brought for me before he died. It was cocaine white and had tinted windows, twenty two inch rims, and a system in it.

When I pulled up to NaNa's house, I beeped the horn. "She better be ready." I said waiting.

When she came out she was rockin' a cute little outfit. She was my closes girl friend, but she often got on my nerves, but she cool though. We've been friends since she moved here in the third grade from Atlanta. She is very pretty and stays rocking the cutest clothes. Her boyfriend Damien is always out hustling to make his money, and that's why she stays fitted. She has her own place across town. Me, I was still living at home with my mom, because of my little rinky dink job working part time at the mall.

"What's up girl?" NaNa said as she got into the car.

"This party. I'm just ready to hit up the club and to get my mind off of what's been going on to the house."

"I feel ya girl. I called Mieko, and he said it's thick in there."

Mieko is another member of the crew. He is mixed between Black and Latino. He's tall, with some cute hazel eyes and a caramel complexion. He was a ladies man and the ladies loved him. We have been friends since I can remember. We grew up just a few blocks away until he moved across town.

"You know it's always jumping in Club X." I cranked the car back up and bumped my music all the way to the club.

When we got there it was indeed packed. Since Aaron's cousin owns the club, he would let us get one of the VIP sections when no one important was there. Aaron is like my big brother, just like Mieko is. He was the first one there for me when my dad was killed. If I needed him, he was always there. He was a little bit shorter than Mieko and brown skinned. He was one of the realest dudes that I ever knew. He takes nothing from nobody, but he is very kind at heart.

I spotted our other friend Marcus, but we always call him Trill. He was out dancing with some girl. Trill is brown skin, about an inch or two taller than me. He sports a grill, dreads and always has a fitted hat tilted to the right side. Even though Trill is not all that tall everybody knows not to mess with him. Ever since the first time we met, he always called me Shawty Red anytime he sees me. He's just as cool as the others. We've been friends since about the tenth grade.

"Shawty Red, NaNa. What's up?"

"Trill what up?"

"What up Trill?" I said as we kept waking to the bar to get a drink. Yeah, I know I'm not quiet old enough, but VIP is always tight with the bartenders. I had another five months before my 21st birthday.

"Hey Beautiful. What you having tonight?" The bartender Frank asked with a smile on his face.

"I'll get a Pineapple Daiquiri."

"What about you Tosha?"

"Same old thing as usual and you know it," NaNa says as she bobbed to the music.

Frank goes and fixed the two drinks and is back very quickly.

"Here you go ladies."

"Thanks Frank."

"Thank you." He winked at me.

Frank always liked me, but he was eight years older than me. He was sexy as hell, but I really couldn't get with the age difference and besides I wasn't ready to talk to anyone yet.

After we got our drinks we went over to the VIP section. There was Mieko, with a girl on his arm and another in his face. Aaron was sitting down with some girl, and he had just lit up a blunt.

"What up yall?" NaNa said as she pulled one of Mieko's girls up out of a seat.

She act like she was about to say something, but I quickly shut that shit down, when I looked at her like I dared her to say something. The girl sucked her teeth and found her another seat.

"Chillin, chillin. What took yall so long?" Mieko asked after taking the blunt form Aaron.

"You know how slow your home girl is." Mieko passes me the blunt, and I take a hit. "How long yall been here?" I pass it to NaNa.

"About like an hour or some shit."

"I'm so fucking blowed though. Ma is getting on my nerves like on some real shit. I'm ready to move up out that bitch. I'm grown right?" Everybody nods, and say yeah. "So why is she still treating me like a little ass girl? That shit is way past old."

"You know you can come stay with me for a while," Mieko says.

"Not with all them bitches you have all running through there."

"If you serious girl, you know you can kick it with me and Damien."

"You good girl. I ain't trying to move in there with you in Damien." I take another sip of my drink.

Aaron says, "Come on Applez, you know you can kick it with me. All you got to do is say it."

"I know Aaron. I might have to do that though, because I can't take this shit anymore."

My favorite song came on and I was ready to get out and dance. I took two more pulls of the blunt and passed it to NaNa. "You coming NaNa?"

"Yeah." She takes a puff of the blunt and passes it to Aaron.

We both leave VIP and go to the dance floor. As I got on the dance floor, I heard somebody call my name.

"Yolanda," a voice called out over the music.

I turned around and it was Jeremy. He was my friend from back in school, he wanted to talk to me, but I was with Ace and at the time he wasn't my type. "Hey Jeremy." We hugged.

"You want to dance with me." He finally makes his way to me getting through the thick crowd.

When we started dancing, I started moving my body to the beat, while Jeremy grinded against me. He wasn't showing any restraint. We were so into the song, you couldn't tell me I wasn't doing my thing right then. I could feel the people looking at us. Jeremy took both of my hands and was holding them up in the air, while I was twerking on him. Then out of nowhere I busted out a split.

"Damn girl," he said.
I came back up, "Can't handle that?"
"You shitting me."

13

We continued to dance through that song. After I had danced my ass off through the next song, I was ready to take a seat. "You want to come over and chill with us?"

"Yeah, that's cool. First I'm going to hit the bar up real quick."

"Alright."

I walk back to the VIP.

"I seen you out there fuckin ole buddy," Trill said as she sits back down.

"Chill out. You can't be talking when you had your hands up that girl skirt feeling on her ass, when we first came in this club."

NaNa comes back over, looking fucked up. I guess that blunt and drinks was getting to her, she never really could manage them both together. "Damn Applez, I seen you out there. Jeremy was all in it."

"Fucked 'em up with that split though." Trill said.

"Yeah I know. Had to show I wasn't playing."

Jeremy comes over to the VIP with two drinks. "Here you go."

"Thank you. This is my last drink of the night because I got to drive my ass back home."

"Well, I know I plan on getting fucked up, and have me a good time," NaNa was talking louder now. "Let Damien beat it out the frame."

"Ain't nobody want to hear that shit," Aaron gets up and the girl that was with him follows and they go out on the floor to dance.

"I'm about to go yall, I got to go handle some business." Mieko gets up grinning as the other two girls get up holding each other's hand.

"Mieko is a straight freak," I stated.

"Shit, you know Mieko. He always fucking something."

"He need to chill out though."

"Jeremy. What you doing back down here, I thought you had moved to Carolina?" asked NaNa.

"Yeah. But I'm moving back some time, because I been ready to come back home. Trying to see what Yolanda been up too."

"Nothing much. Shit you know me stay coolin it. Trying to keep these hater."

"For real though," NaNa gave me some dap.

"Yall two are still the same."

"Ain't no reason to change," I said.

A dude had walked over to NaNa. "What up lil ma, you wanna dance?"

"Yep." She gets up, "I'll be back girl.", and goes back onto the dance floor. Now Jeremy and I were the only ones there sitting down.

"So what's up with you and your girl?"

"I wish I knew."

"What you mean by that?" I take another sip of my drink.

"She acts fucking crazy sometimes. She thinking I'm cheating on her, but I'm not."

"I thought everything was good with you two?"

"I did too, until she started trippin. I'm telling you I'm about to leave her crazy ass in Carolina and move back and just forget her."

I begin to laugh.

"You said you still doing your thang?"

"Yeah, still single and loving every minute of it. I don't have to be tied down to nobody." I finish the rest of my drink. "You need to get like me."

"Shit. I can't keep up with you." He laughs.

"So, when are you going back?" I ask.

"Sunday night."

"Why so early?"

"I remember one time you ain't want me in your face talking to you, but now you worried about when I'm going back?"

I roll my eyes. "Not with this shit again Jey."

"Back when we were sophomores, I asked you to be my girl and you straight dogged me right in front of my boys."

"You needed to grow up. You and all your little friends always were childish, and wonder why being such a pretty boy, why a lot of girls didn't want yall."

Jeremy laughs. "Yeah, well I'm leaving Monday."

"Oh. How long you been down here?"

"Since yesterday."

"Aww, you got to get back to your girl?"

"Yeah, before she come calling me. Aye but let me get your number so we can stay up."

"Alright. Let me see your phone."

He pulls his phone out of his pocket and gives it to me, and I give him mines. I put his number in my phone, and give it back. Jeremy was taking a little too long with my phone.

"What you doing?"

"Looking at your pictures."

"No. Give me my phone." I reached for my phone trying to take it away from him, because I knew I had some picture only I knew about in it, well, maybe one other person I was just talking to for a while.

"Damn girl." He looks at my pictures amazed. "Send this to my phone."

"Hell no," still trying to get my phone, but I finally gave up.

"Who took this picture?" He turned the phone to me to see.

"Don't worry about it."

He keeps looking at the pictures until he sees them all, and gives me back my phone. Jeremy looks at me and starts smiling. There was defiantly something cooking up, so I had to turn my head to the crowd. I started giggling. "Oh boy."

"What?"

"Nothing...Nothing." I shake my head as I look back at him.

Another song that we liked came on and we went back to dance. Everybody was singing along to the song, When it went off they played a slower song. Now we were slow dancing with each other.

This moment reminded me of the time of our junior prom. We went as friends, but hooked up after words. *Damn that shit was good*, but we knew it couldn't be no more than just that one time because we knew it wouldn't work out. When he moved to South Carolina we really didn't get to talk very much. I'll spot him every now and then down here, but never got a chance to really talk to him.

"Hey, you remember that time we went to prom in the eleventh grade."

"Yeah," he replied. "How could I forget?"

"That was a nice day. You were looking so good." I responded looking into his eyes.

"That dress you wore though. Man. You was fitting that nicely."

"Yeah I know." I smile giggling. "What about afterwards?"

"I won't ever forget that. We were supposed to go to that party at the club afterwards, but we made other plans."

"And when you brought me home, my mom and dad was so pissed at me for not coming home on time. That night was worth it though."

"Was it?" He smiled.

I nodded my head.

"So how are you and your mom anyway?"

"Worst. You know how she got after dad was murdered. I don't think she'll ever be the same." I look away from him. "Life will never be like it was before then. Me and her was cool. Now all we do is get into it with each other."

"You always should hope for the better."

I thought about what Jeremy said for a min. The song finally ends and I was ready to go.

"I got to be getting back home. I ain't trying to hear mama mouth tonight, so just call me before you leave."

"I will." He gives me a hug.

"See you Jeremy. Now, I got to go look for NaNa."

"Alright." He look at me and licks his lips as I walk off.

I head over to the bar to go see if Frank seen NaNa.

"Have you seen NaNa?"

"Yeah she's over there."

"Thanks."

I start to walk off, but stops when Frank says, "You about to leave?"

"Yeah."

"You going to be back tomorrow?"

"I don't know. I might if I'm not busy."

"Alright. I'll see you then."

"Bye."

I get up off the stool and go over to NaNa. She was dancing with some tall dude, had to be about 6'2". Under his ass, shit we both looked like midgets.

"Come on girl, I'm about to leave."

"Alright Applez. I'll be to the car in a minute."

"No, you can come right now."

I grab NaNa by the arm, and we go to the car. She was drunk. Even though she only had a few drinks, you couldn't tell the difference. Whenever she gets drunk, she gets a little too friendly, so I have to watch out for my girl.

"Damn girl. You just pulled me up off of that cutie like that."

"Me and you both know Damien will kill his ass and maybe even yours even if you thought of giving him your number."

"Yeah, you right."

19

We get into the car and exit the parking lot. On the way home all I could think about was Jeremy. *'What would it be like if we did get together?' 'Would he have changed my life for the best?'*

After I dropped off NaNa I went back home. As soon as I got there, my mom was there with the arguing.

"Where in the hell were you at?"

"Why do you need to know?" I try walking up stairs to my room.

"Don't talk back to me. Where were you? You supposed to be home at one," she says as she stumbles to her feet, from the couch.

"I am a grown ass woman. So you cannot give me no type of damn curfew. I ain't no damn baby anymore."

"If you are so gown, get your ass out of my house. We not having two grown women in one house."

"Forget this. I don't need to stay here, and I damn sure don't need you telling me what to do. Ever since daddy was killed all you do is drink. Do you think that bottle is going to bring him back? Because it damn sure ain't."

Once I said that my mom slapped me in the face. It shocked me, because she had never hit me a day in her life.

"Get your shit and get out of my god damn house."

I ran up to my room and pack an overnight bag, because I wasn't going to stay there that night, and would just have Aaron to bring me back for the rest of my stuff when she wasn't home tomorrow. Aaron was the only person I could count on in a situation like this. It's been many nights that I had to go over to his house to get some rest from my mom, but today was the last I was taking this from her.

"Seeing that you want me gone, don't expect me back but to get my clothes. I'm moving out this house." I walk to the door, open it and slam it.

As I got in the car, I couldn't help but break down into tears. I had reached my breaking point. I called up Aaron to let him know I was on my way.

"What up?"

Sniffling and barely getting my words out I say, "Can I come stay at your house tonight?"

"Yeah."

"I'll tell you about it when I get there."

"Alright."

I end the call, crank the car up and burn out from the house. I didn't want to live there anymore, and that was my last day.

I get out of the car and go to Aaron's apartment and knock on the door. It wasn't long before he answered.

"Another fight with your Ms. Faith?"

We walk into his place.

"Yeah. She told me to pack my shit and get out her house." The tears start back falling down my face. Aaron, being the brotherly type, wraps his arms around me and holds me. He knows all the pain I've been through, he's been my best friend for a long time, and if it was anybody I could trust, he was defiantly the one.

"Why is my life like this? Everything is so fucked up it don't make no since." He lets go of me and we sit down in the living room.

"You know you can stay with me for however long you have to. My place is yours."

Chapter 2

The next morning when I woke up I made sure my mom wasn't home before I decided to go get the rest of my clothes.

"Did you sleep alright?"

"No. I couldn't sleep." I slept in Aaron's extra room that night, and couldn't sleep for shit. When I finally did, it didn't take long before I was awake again.

"When you have to go back to work?"

"I don't have to go until tomorrow afternoon." I say as I put another bag into the car. "I'm going out again tonight, but leaving early like eleven."

"I might hang up early too, but I'm not going to the club." He puts my last bag into his all black Cadillac Escalade.

"You don't have to stay in because of me."

"I wasn't planning on staying out long either tonight, because I got to go to work in the morning."

"Oh." I close's his back hatch down, and then we get into his truck.

"I don't want to have to be depending on you to have some place to stay, so as soon as possible I'm look for a place. With all the money I've been saving and the money my dad had saved up for me."

"Like I said it ain't a problem, but I'll help you find a place if you want me to."

"Thank you."

Aaron cranks up and drives off.

When we finally get back, we put up all of my stuff in the room. I had to call NaNa and tell her everything that had went down after the club.

"Oh, what up Applez?"

"Noting much. Just calling to let you know I'm moving out mama house."

"What happened?"

"When I walked in the door she already asking me where I've been and talking it was pass my curfew."

"Curfew?"

"Yeah. I was like I ain't no little girl and I don't need a curfew. I was like I am a grown ass woman. She told me two grown women can live under one roof, and told me to get my shit and get out, so I left. Now I'm at Aaron's. Are you coming by?"

There is knocks at the door, and Aaron goes and answer, and its Mieko.

"What up man?" Mieko says. "What up Applez?"

"Nothing much. Same old shit," Aaron replies.

I give him a nod of the head, and start back talking to NaNa.

"Who that?"

"Mieko."

"I might be over there later."

"Alright. So yall did what you said?"

"Me and Damien?"

"Yeah."

"Girl yes. Soon as I got in the house, he was home, and I jumped his ass."

I start laughing.

"I'm telling you we fucked so many times last night. The shit was incredible. I mean that's why I'm like just getting up."

"Yall is so freakin wild."

"I'll call you back later though girl."

"Alright."

"Bye," I end the call and then go sit over where Mieko and Aaron were.

"That shit that went down last night was crucial. I ain't never had that shit done before." Mieko starts talking about the night he had with the two girls that he had in VIP.

"What happened?"

"Them chicks I left the club with came back to my place, and before we could get in the door good both of 'em was on me. That dark skinned one gave me head so good, man shit I'm telling you. While she was doing that other girl was eating her out. I sat back and watch them do they thang. So, ole girl game over and took a condom off my dresser and put it on with her mouth. No hands used."

Aaron gives him some dap. "Damnit man."

"Yall is disgusting."

"Anyways, then the brown skinned one jumped on my dick and started riding. She was facing my feet, so the other one got at the other end of the bed and laid down and the brown skinned chick ate her out as she was riding my dick."

"Dem bitches is nasty as fuck."

"Talented. That shit they were doing. Ooowee."

"For real," Aaron says.

"Yall stupid. I'm about to go wash."

"You going to let me get in with you?" Mieko joked.

"Hell no." I get up and go take a shower. When I was done I got dressed. I had on some leggings and a cute blouse, then I did my hair and left out.

"Where you going?" Aaron asked.

"I'm just about to go out for a few. I'll be back."

"Alright."

"Damn Applez. You look good," Mieko said standing up.

"Yeah." I open the door and headed outside. I got into my car, cranked it up, and head over to the mall. Shopping always comforted me.

When I got there I went straight to the shoe store, because I love sneakers. I looked around and bought about three pair. As I walked out of that sore, I bumped into Frank.

"Hey Applez."

"Oh what's up Frank?"

"Just out buying some shit."

"Me too."

"So, you coming to the club tonight right?"

"Yeah I'm going to be there , but I'm leaving early."

"Ok. Hey can I get your number so I can call you sometime?"

"Yeah, I guess so." I took his phone from him and put my number in it.

"So what's a good time for me to call you?"

"Anytime really. If I don't answer right then, I'll call you or text back."

"Alright. I guess I'll see you tonight."

"Ok."

Frank was really feeling me, and he always tried to talk to me. Yeah he was cute, but the age difference was my biggest problem. I thought I should at least talk to him and give him a try if everything was alright.

I continued shopping and went back to the house afterwards.

*   *   *

"Let me get a..." I was saying before I was cut off by Frank.

"Ciroc." He says as he takes the seat next to me at the bar.

I smiled. "I thought you had to work tonight."

"I took off tonight."

"So you only work Thursday thru Sunday at nights?"

"Yeah. This is just a side job I do to pass over some time. The rest of the time, I'm helping my cousin run a little business."

"Oh, that's good." The bartender gives me my drink and I drink some and place it back down.

"What about you? You still work in the mall?"

"Yeah. I want to find some other place to work though."

"You look good tonight. Not like you don't look good every day."

I had on an all-black dress with some heels on. "Thank you. I have to say you looking good too."

"I try to," He said as he smiled at me. "You knew tonight was slow jams night right?"

"Yeah I did. I'm more than about shaking my ass."

"My bad, I didn't mean it like that. I've seen you at other spots."

"Oh have you?"

"Yeah. I saw you across town at Dapper's one day."

"Why you never said anything." I took another sip of my drink.

"Didn't want to bother you."

"You wouldn't have."

"Well can I get that dance now then?"

"I don't want to leave my drink up here."

"That's ok. I'll buy you another one."

He took my hand and brought me to the dance floor and took me into his arms. I just followed his step and we began to dance. Through the first part we didn't say anything. It felt really relaxing being in his arms. I hadn't been in another man's arms like this in a while. I actually kind of liked it. His body against mine was what I needed.

"This feels good," I said while laying my head on his chest. "I haven't felt this relaxed in a long time."

"As young as you are, I feel sorry for you sometimes when you are going through the stuff you do. I hate to see pain on your pretty little face."

"Sometimes I wish I wasn't ever born into this. A lot of people think I'm cocky or stuck up, but they have no idea about the stuff I go through."

"I feel the same too, but I just got to play my cards like they were dealt."

"Yeah," I drag out with a sigh.

Frank grabs my face and turns it to him and he gives me a kiss on the lips. It was soft, but yet so powerful. He took me by surprise. He finally drops his hand from my chin.

"I've always wanted to do that."

He looks down at me to see my reaction, but I couldn't say anything. All I could do is stare back at him, and to wonder why again was it that I didn't ever give him any play. Age really wasn't anything but a number. I just laid my head back down on his chest and continued to dance.

Afterwards he brought me a drink and we sat and talked a while about lots of things. Like our family and our future. Come to find out, this dude was really interesting.

"I got to be getting home now. I guess I'll see you some other time." I say.

"I was wondering could we go on a date next Saturday."

"I'll have to think about it, but I'll call you and let you know."

"Alright. See you later."

I get off the bar stool and run my hand across his back. "See you later." I walk off and went to my car and left to go back to Aaron's.

"What yall been doing?" I asks.

"Chillin really," Mieko answers.

"Why you looking so happy?" Aaron asked.

"Oh nothing. I just had a good time. Frank and I was just talking and we danced a few times."

"Frank. I thought you ain't like that nigga," Mieko said.

"We sat and we talked, and I figured out he is kind of cool. He asked me to go on a date with him Saturday after next," I said as I took off my shoes.

"You going?" asked Aaron.

"I don't know. I told him I'll call him."

Aaron shakes his head at me, because he knew how I said I felt about Frank, and now he couldn't understand why I was feeling the way I'm was feeling now. He wanted me to be happy, but why Frank?

"I'm about to take a shower. I'll be right back."

"Alright."

I went to the room to get some clothes. I still could smell Frank's cologne on me. It smelled really good. I got my pajamas out my bag and went to the bathroom to take my shower. All I could think about was how Frank kissed me. I enjoyed our night together. I wanted to go on a date with him, so I can try the dating again. When I finished I went back to the living room.

They had the TV on the news and they news lady was talking about a wreck on my mom's side of town.

"Aaron you'll turn that up a little bit." I say as I remain standing watching TV.

'This is Channel 6 reporting live from Bakers St. on the Westside. There has been a major car wreck and we don't know the extent of the injuries, but it looks very rough out here. A car collided into a pickup truck. The car seems to be totaled, and the fire department is trying their best to get the person inside out. The only other information that we have is it seems to be a young black woman inside with a license plate that says ICE.'

"Oh my god, that's my mama."

Chapter 3

Aaron and Mieko had to calm me down, because I got so frantic that I didn't know what to do. We all into Aaron's truck and rushed down to where the car accident was. Indeed it was my mom's car and it didn't look good. Aaron found the nearest parking spot and we down to the accident site.

"Let me in. That's my mom in there."

Police officers were holding me back from seeing if she was alright.

"No I can't let you go through there."

I stood back crying as they cut the top off of my mom's car with the Jaws of Life. Aaron and Mieko came and stood with me. Aaron wrapped his arms around me. When they finally got the top off, a paramedic tried to find a pulse but couldn't. He shook his head and then I knew that was the last I would have a mother.

When I saw that notion I fell into Aaron's arms. I couldn't watch them pull my mother from the car and put her on the stretcher to take her away. I ran back over to the car and got inside. Mieko and Aaron run behind me.

"I shouldn't have ever said all I said to her. Now she's gone. I can't...I can't go through this shit anymore." I leaned over to Aaron and put my arms around him.

The police office that stopped us at the caution tape came over to the car, and knocked on the window.

I stepped out of the car.

"I'm so sorry for your loss. By the look of things, we could smell a heavy odor of alcohol on your mom, and she probably lost control of the vehicle and crashed. Is there anything we can do to help you?"

"No. I just want to go home."

"Can I get your phone number so we can call you to give you any more information?"

"Yeah." I give him my number and he leaves.

"Come on Applez, I'll drive," Mieko says.

Mieko get out the car and get in the driver seat while Aaron and me get in the back.

"You sure you ok," Aaron ask.

"Yeah. I know this might sound fucked up, but it's honest. She's better off dead, than to suffer like she has been doing since daddy was killed. At least now she is with him."

I called my Auntie Lisa to let her know everything, and she said she was going to try to make it

33

in by tonight. Aunt Lisa is my mother's only sister. After all the crying on the phone, she finally hangs up. I called NaNa and she meets us over to Aaron's place.

We all sit around and talk for a while. NaNa and Mieko stays over at Aaron's with me, but I had to get away. So, when I thought everybody was sleep I left and went out to the park to sit by the lake to just sit and think.

"You always did come out here when you were mad or had something on your mine," Aaron came up behind me and sat down on the bench.

"Yeah."

"I know exactly how you feeling though. I remember when my mom passed away when I was eleven from doing drugs. I was right there when she had overdosed. That shit fucks with me till this day."

I remembered that day too. Aaron was so heart broke. He had to go live with his grandparents after that. Growing up he used to get into so much trouble, but he changed after his grandma got sick.

"Plus your mama and daddy was always my second family, so I'm hurting just like you."

We sat for an hour or so just silent and looking out across the water. Even though we said nothing, we could tell what each other were thinking.

"You ready to go now?"

"Yeah." Me and Aaron got up and we walked to our cars and went back to his house.

Around two o' clock the next day I woke up to my phone ringing. I looked at it and it was Jeremy. I really didn't feel like talking to anybody that morning, but I answered the phone anyway.

"Hello," I said with a weak voice.

"Yolanda?"

"Yeah, this me."

"Why you sound like that?"

"I been up all night, and you woke me up."

"I can call you back later if you want me too."

"No you cool."

"Having trouble with your mom again?"

"Something like that." I take a pause. "She was in a wreck last night."

"Is she alright." He as seriously concerned

"No. She died."

"I'm sorry to hear about that. Where are you at right now?"

"At Aaron's house."

"Are you ok?"

"Yeah." I roll over onto my stomach.

"Can I come see you or something?"

"I thought you were going back home today?"

"I can leave later."

"Why would you do that for me?"

"We are friends right?"

"Yeah."

"I'll be over there to get you in a minute."

"Ok. I got to get ready."

"Alright."

"Bye."

"Bye." I hang up the phone and get up and get dressed. I put my hair up into a bun. I could hear everybody in the living room talking, so I went into the living room.

"Hey Applez," NaNa said. "You ok?"

"Yeah I'm good." I said taking a seat between Aaron and Mieko.

"Jeremy is supposed to come by and see me. I just got off the phone with him."

"Oh," NaNa said.

"Yeah."

NaNa could tell I was getting ready to tear up. "Everything will be ok Applez."

I shook my head and said, "No it's not going to be ok. I don't care how angry we were at each other. I'm not going to get my mama back. It's tearing me up that the last moment I had with her was of us arguing and me cursing at her and none of that shit is sitting well with me." I got up and went outside. I sat on the trunk of my car crying until Jeremy came up. He pulled up right beside me in his car.

"You ok Yolanda?"

I wiped away my tears and looked up. He got out of his car and came over to me.

"I was just in my feelings about what went down the last time I talked to my mama."

"Come here." I get down and go to him and he hugs me.

"Can we just leave here?" I say.

"Yeah. Have you ate yet?"

"No."

"I'll take you to get some breakfast." Jeremy opens the door to his car, and I get in. Then he comes around the other side and get in.

Jeremy drives to IHOP. When we get there we get out and take a booth. Soon as we sit down his phone rings and he answers it and it was his girlfriend. When he gets off the phone he starts shaking his head.

"What?" I pick up a menu.

"She want to know why I ain't called her, and why I ain't on my way yet.

"Oh."

"All this bullshit, I know it won't be much longer before this is a done deal. I'm trying to work things out, but she not doing her part."

"Well, you got to do what you got to do."

A waiter comes over.

"May I take your orders?"

"Yeah, can I get the pancakes and sausage?" He writes down the order.

"Let me get the same thing," Jeremy replies.

"Ok." The waiter leaves.

Jeremy looks me over. "Damn. You are so beautiful."

"Thank you, but I know I'm looking rough right now."

"You still look beautiful to me though."

I smile. "You already know what I think about you."

"Yeah." He starts looking at me and grin.

The waiter comes back with our food and my phone goes and it was my Auntie Lisa.

"Hello."

"Hey this Auntie Lisa."

"Hey Auntie." I take a drink of my orange juice.

"How you doing?"

37

"I'm alright," I say in a sadden voice.

"Are you at the house?"

"No ma'am, I'm out eating breakfast with a friend."

"I'm on my way to the house right now. Me Michael and the kids."

"I'll be there after I get finished eating."

"I'll call you when we get there."

"Alright." I hang up my phone and sit it on the table. "That was my Auntie, she says she is on the way to the house, but honestly, I don't want to go."

"But you know you got to go. That's your family," Jeremy says as he pours some syrup onto his pancake and sausage.

"Yeah." I paused. "Can you drop me off by there, after we leave from here? I'll get one of my cousins to drive me to Aaron's."

"Yeah." He looks up from taking a sip of his orange juice.

We eat our food, but I wasn't really much hungry, so I still had food on my plate.

"Something wrong?" Jeremy asks curiously.

"No. I'm just ready to go. I'm not hungry anymore." My phone rings and it's my Auntie again. She tells me that she made it to the house and that my Auntie Cynthia (my mom's stepsister), my cousin Jasmine, and Uncle Ryan are also coming. I tell her we we'll be there in fifteen minutes.

Me and Jeremy gets up and pay for the food and leave. Our ride home was pretty much quiet beside the radio playing.

When we get there he pulls next to the curb in front of the house.

"I'll call you when I get back home," Jeremy said as I opened the car door to get out.

"Alright. Thanks for today."

"It's all good. You ain't going to come give me a hug?"

"You going to get out?"

Jeremy gets out and rounds the car over to me. He gives me a hug, and holds onto my waist.

"Drive safe."

"I will." He gives me a kiss on the lips. "See you later." He lets go of me and get into his car and drive off leaving me standing there.

As I walk up the steps, the door opens and my cousin Jasmine comes outside with a cigarette in hand. "Hey Jasmine." Jasmine is a year older than me, and ever since we were younger, we could never stand each other.

"Yolanda." She says with attitude. She is one of the few who still calls me by my real name. And as you can tell, we still don't get along.

I continue into the house and people are in the living room. I go to find my Auntie Lisa.

*   *   *

The funeral was held the Saturday after the accident. It was a nice home going for my mother. I cried so much leading up to the funeral, that I couldn't shed another tear. When it came time for reflections from the family and friends, I went up and spoke.

"I want to thank everyone for attending my mother's services. As all of you know, I've been in this exact place eight years ago for my father's home going. It hurts a lot to not have either one of them here with me, but what hurts the most as that me and my mom never hashed out our problems that we had before she died. I cried day in and day out about it, but I decided there was no need to cry anymore and I prayed to God for my forgiveness, so I cried my last tears yesterday."

I started to sing Mary Mary's song yesterday. After the first chorus the pianist played the song and the people in the church joined in with me.

After the funeral everyone went back to my mom's house, but I left and came back to Aaron's house.

The next weekend I decided not to mope around and to just go out.

"I'm about to go out to the club, yall coming?" I ask.

Mieko replies, "I got this girl I need to get up with real quick. See what she got going on."

"Do you ever get tired?" I laugh.

"I don't ever get tired of the pussy."

"I got to go to work in the morning, so I'm staying in tonight," says Aaron.

"Well, I guess I'll go out by myself, since NaNa wit Damien. I'll see yall later tonight." I pick up my purse and keys and head to the door. When I got in the car I took my cell phone out of my purse and called Frank.

"Hello," he answers.

"Hey, this Applez." I start my car up and backed out of the parking spot and get out on the road.

"Oh what's up?"

"I was wondering was you working tonight."

"No I'm off tonight, but I'll come through if you want me too."

"Yeah, I would like to see you there."

"Well I'll be there soon."

"Alright." I hang the phone up, and go to the club. When I get there, about ten minutes later Frank comes and makes his way over to me.

"Hey," I greet him.

"How you doing?"

"I'm good. The funeral was what was to be expected. I just had to leave them back at mama house. I had to get out of that element."

He takes a seat next to me. "You want a drink?"

"Mine as well."

"What you having today?"

"You should already know." I look at him.

"Can I get a Pineapple Daquiri for the lady, and let me get a shot of grey goose." He told Daniel the bartender.

"You looking good tonight." I say smiling.

"You too."

"Thank you."

"After your drink you want to dance?"

"Yeah, we can do that." The bartender comes back with the drinks. "Thank you." I drink some of my drink.

"Are we still going out tomorrow?"

"Yeah, if anything doesn't come up."

41

We keep talking and have another drink and then we get on the dance floor. When I moved, Frank was right there with me. He was a good dancer. After two dances, we went back to the bar for another drink.

"I didn't know you could dance like that."

"Yeah, I got a lot more talents than just dancing."

"Oh, is that right?" I say with a smirk.

"Yeah. That's right," he smiles back.

"Ok." I drink some more of my drink, and sit it back down at the bar.

We drink and talk some more. Until Keith Sweat's song "A Wrong and a Right Way" comes on.

We stood near the wall and vibed to the music. I stood infront of him and sung the song.

"I didn't know you could sing?"

"Just a little bit. It ain't nothing special."

"I like it though."

"You want me to sing to you?" I raised my eyebrow.

He nodded his head yeah, so I sung the rest of the song to him. I put on a little show for him.

We stared into each other's eyes and the next thing you know we were kissing. At the moment I was really feeling him. I don't know if it was the alcohol or what.

"Do you have anything else planned for tonight?"

"No. Why you ask?" I say shaking my head.

"Would you like to come over for some alone time?"

"That's cool with me."

"Do you want to leave now?"

"Yeah."

I follow Frank outside.

"Just stay behind me, and I'll lead you to my house."

I get in the car, crank up, and follow Frank. In my mind, if anything happens, it just happens. I hadn't been with a guy in over seven months now, so I'm really ready for whatever may happen.

I start to notice that we were going across town to the upper class neighborhoods. I knew good and well, a little job with a cousin is not making enough money to live out here, but I'm not asking any questions right now. When we arrived to his place, it was a big two story house.

I get out when we get there. "So, this is your house?"

"Yeah."

"Well, I see where the money is at."

He laughs.

We walk up to the house and he unlocks the door, and we go inside.

It was very pretty inside, with two lion statues as you enter the foyer and it was a fountain in the middle. Then we went into the living room. It was a big screen TV in there with another set of surveillance TVs. We sit down on the couch.

"I love your house."

"Yeah. I saved up and got this. It took a minute though. I've been living here for three years now, but with nobody to share it with."

"So you never had any candidates?"

"Not really. Not anyone that I thought truly deserved it."

I nodded my head.

"Do you want me to fix you a drink?"

I shouldn't have another, because I already have a little buzz going on, but hey. "Yeah."

He gets up and tells me to come with him to the kitchen. When we get there, he has an island in the middle of the floor, and all of the counter tops are made of marble. He has a huge refrigerator, and all the appliances are silver.

I take a seat on a stool and watch him fix me and him another drink. "Here you go."

"What time is it?"

"It's just 12:43, you need to be somewhere, or something?"

"Oh no, I was just asking." I drink some more of my drink.

"Can I tell you something?"

I put my drink down. "Yeah."

"I'm really feeling you, and I have been for a while. It's just everything about you. Your walk, your talk, your style, I like everything about you."

"Thank you." I start blushing.

"Do you ever think we can make something out of this? I really like you. I know we got an age difference, but that really don't mean anything. I mean we been knowing each other for a few years now. And I can tell you whatever you need to know about me."

I shake my head yeah. "Yes I would like to get to know more about you, and the possibility is there that something can come from this."

Frank comes and stands in front of me and we kissed. It was so intense. I stand up and wrap my arms around his neck. He put his hand against the side of my face, and then run it over my shoulder and down my back. The next thing you know I'm standing there with my shirt and bra off. His tone body was pressed up against my hard nipples and his warm body felt so good up against me. I know he could feel the heat of my body rise. I lift my head up and he starts kissing on my neck, and I moan. He picks me up and I wrap my legs tightly around his waist.

He takes me up stairs to his room and corners me into a wall and continues kissing me. He pulls off my pants and my thongs slide down as well. He takes off all of his clothes. I didn't know his body was so built with an eight pack and some nice muscles. He reaches into a draw right beside us and pulls out a condom and put it on. He lifts me up against the wall, and slowly slides me down onto him. I let out a high moan as he goes inside of me. Being only in this sex game for a little while, it was kind of painful taking all of him, but he made sure he took his time with me. He slowly moves up and down, and then he begins to pick up speed. He keeps going until he makes my body quiver.

From there he took me to the bed and laid me down. He stood up straight and started kissing down my legs until his face reached my pussy, and he began to eat me so good.

"How that feel?" He says in the most seductive voice you would ever want to here.

"Mm. It feels so good."

"I want you to tell me when to stop."

"Don't stop. Keep going."

He starts licking harder and faster. I was getting so weak now. He takes his tongue and put it deep into me, rubbing all over my body.

"Just like that," I cry out.

He keeps at it until he makes me cum for the third time. Then he goes back inside me and does me so good. He knew exactly what he was doing. I was taking in every inch of him. His strokes were slow and deep and I was loving it.

He begins licking and sucking on my breast, squeezing hard, and caressing my body. He picks my left leg up and starts sucking on my toes while still stroking. Everything he was doing was feeling so good. It was long before I came again

I was breathing heavily.

He bends down and kiss me. "Come here," He gets from off of me and lies on his back and then I climb on top and start riding. I could barely take it. He pulled me down to his chest and held on tight, increasing the feeling. I slow grind on top of him until we both erupt.

Chapter 4

"Good morning," I was awaked by Frank's voice.

My head was pounding from the drinking, but I could remember everything that went down last night. "Morning," I let out with a groan.

"How you feel?"

"My head is killing me and I'm so tired. What time is it?

"12:15," he says as he sits on the bed next to me and turn the TV to the news.

I sit up and rub my temples. "Do you have some aspirin?"

"Yeah they are in the medicine cabinet in the bathroom. I'll get it for you."

"No, I'll get it. I have to use the bathroom anyway."

"I put your clothes in the chair over there."

I get up, get my clothes and go to the bathroom to take an aspirin and to wash up. I wash put on my clothes then go back to the bedroom where Frank is at.

"I had a great time with you last night, but I need to be getting back."

"Ok, I'll walk you outside."

"Ok." I turn to his bedroom door and go out down the stairs and to the front door.

"Thank you for last night. I'll call you later, or either you can call me." Frank says to me.

"Alright." I give him a kiss on the cheek then leave. I check my phone, and Aaron and NaNa had called my phone. I knew Aaron was gone to work, so I wasn't going to bother calling him.

I go to Aaron's house to change. After I took a shower and put on my clothes, I called NaNa.

"Hello," NaNa answered.

"I was calling you back since you called me last night." I sit down on a chair in the kitchen while I poured me some orange juice.

"Aaron called me last night looking for you, so I called you and you didn't answer. Where was your ass at?"

"Well, Frank met me at the club since he didn't have to work last night. We were drinking, dancing and having a good time. After a while he invited me back to his house, we talked, had another drink or two, then we had sex." I was very blunt.

"Wait a minute. Frank? Bartender Frank? Hold on, I thought you wasn't feeling him?"

"I thought I wasn't either, but girl he is amazing."

"I know you going to tell me about it."

"Yeah. Since yall was busy I called him up last night to go out with me. After we had some drinks and danced, he invited me back to his place to talk. You should see his house, it's big and beautiful."

"Where he live?"

"He lives in The Elks and you know you got to have money to stay out there. He was telling me how he was feeling me and I told him I was feeling him too. He said did I want to make something out of this and I said yeah and from there we started kissing. In a matter of seconds my shirt and bra was off he takes me up stairs to his room. He posted me up against the wall and we fucked so magically." I drink some of my juice.

NaNa giggles.

"So, then he laid me down on the bed and he I found out how good his tongue game was. It was so good till he had me weak. Then we went back at it."

"I still can't believe that you hooked up with Frank, of all people. I ain't mad at you though."

"But guess who else is feeling me even though they got a girl."

"Who girl?"

"Jeremy."

"What?"

"Yes, the other day when he dropped me off he gave me a kiss and everything."

"You got all the attention, I'm jealous."

"I thought you said Damien was enough man for you?"

"Oh, he is. So does this mean that you and Frank are together?"

"I don't know. I guess."

"Mm."

My phone beeps and I saw I had an incoming call from Jeremy.

"I'll call you back, somebody calling me."

"Ok girl."

I switched over to answer the call. "Hello."

"Hey Yolanda."

"Hey Jeremy." I got to the living room and sit down.

"What you doing?"

"Nothing much. You?"

"I'm chilling to the house by myself."

"Same here."

"Ok. I've been thinking about you."

"Oh really?"

"Yeah."

"I know it's all of a sudden, but I just started talking to somebody right now, and I ain't trying to lead you on in any kind of way."

"Oh ok. That's straight, but all I was saying is that I was thinking about you."

"Oh. What were you thinking about then?"

"That kiss."

"You just left real quick afterwards. I was like well damn, he could of at least said bye."

"I was feeling that though."

"Yeah it was cool."

"Don't front girl. You know you liked it too. I know you felt that."

"It doesn't matter if I felt anything, because you have a girlfriend and like I said I'm talking to someone now."

"Well, I ain't going to bother you no more about that. So, how your day been going so far?"

"It's been cool, kind of tired though."

"Had a long night?"

"Yeah, I just got in really."

"Oh."

I could tell Jeremy was thinking into that statement.

"Well, I was just calling checking up on you. I'll hit you up later though."

"Alright."

After we hung up I decided to go over to NaNa house since it wasn't much to do at Aaron's.

"Hey girl," NaNa greeted me at the door. We went in to sit down in the living room.

"What up? What was you and Damien so wrapped up in yesterday that you couldn't go out?"

"You know he was getting his business right, and after that we was doing what you and Frank was doing."

"Shut up," I roll my eyes.

"Really though, was it good?" Being a bit nosy, as always.

51

"If you must know girl it was too good. His body is just perfect. He got some nice abs, and his tongue game is the truth," I say smiling and giggling.

"He done had his face all in your coochie, I, can't look at him the same anymore." She joked

I laugh. "Whatever. We are supposed to be going out tomorrow. We planned that before any of this happened. I bumped into him when we were both out at the mall one day."

"Ok. I ain't mad at you. It's about time you get you a dude after what happened before."

NaNa was referring to a boyfriend that I had before the time when me and Jeremy went to prom together. His name was Michael, but everyone called him Ace. We were together from sixth grade up until the tenth grade when he was shot one day by a stray bullet at the basketball court down from his house. He died later that night from complications from the gunshot wound. I was in a depression for a little, because it hurt me to my heart to lose the person that I planned to spend the rest of my life with.

NaNa continued talking, "I did thought you and Jeremy were going to get together, but I see nothing happened."

I never did tell anyone, not even NaNa that me and Jeremy did 'hook up' after the prom. All she knows is that I got sick, and Jeremy didn't go to the party after prom because he didn't want to go without me.

"He was too childish. The only reason I went to prom with him, was because it was a last minute thing," I lied. Although he had his childish ways back then, I did like Jeremy, but I hid my true feelings, because I was so use to men in my life not being there anymore.

"But he was and still is fine."

"Yeah," I say nonchalantly.

So we sit and talk and watch TV and continue to talk off and on about Frank. We neither knew much about him, other than he worked at Club X from time to time.

Around 5:30 pm I was still at NaNa's house when Jeremy called back.

"What up?"

"Nothing . I'm over to NaNa's chillin with her." I say looking at NaNa making kissy faces at me. "Stop stupid."

"What?" Jeremy thought I was talking to him.

"Oh I was talking to NaNa." Now she was being childish.

"Let me go outside real quick. Hold on." I get up and go outside to sit on the stoop, away from NaNa. "Yeah I'm back."

"Yeah."

"Where your girl at?"

"She here sleep. She works night shift so she'll be sleep till like ten."

"You are crazy," I laugh.

"How?"

"You already say she think you be cheating on her, now you on the phone with me. What if she not really sleep and listening to you talking?"

"That's her problem. If she listening that's her."

"You are crazy," I say while laughing.

"I know."

"You must be didn't have to work today?"

"No I didn't."

"Yall must hardly ever get time to be together since you work during the day after you get out of school, then she have to go in at night?"

"Hardly, that's one reason why we are like we are."

"I see." I kick a piece of paper of the step. "You never told me what you do besides go to school."

"I work part time with my uncle's company, cleaning office buildings. Trying to safe every penny that I can, even if it's not much."

"I feel ya"

My phone beeps on the other end and it's Frank. "Somebody on the other line, could I call you back some other time?"

"Alright I'll get at you."

"Bye." I switch over to Frank. "Hello," I say happily.

"Hey Applez. How you doing?"

"Oh, I'm good. Real good."

"I was calling to see where you wanted to go out eat at tomorrow."

"Wherever you plan will be fine with me."

"I'll take you to this spot over here."

"Ok. What time will you be coming to get me?"

"Eight."

"Ok. I'll be ready."

"I'll call you back tomorrow. Someone is at the door."

"Ok. Bye."

"Bye."

I go back into the house where NaNa is at. She was still in the living room watching TV.

"What was yall talking about?" she asked.

"Nothing really. I just got off the phone with Frank, and he was telling me where we are going out to eat at."

"Oh ok."

"Well, I'm about to get home and rest some, because I'm still a little sore."

"Oh, that's why you walking like that," being funny.

"Yeah girl." We both start laughing as I start rubbing my stomach. "I worked some muscles I ain't even know about."

"You need to stop it."

"I'll see you tomorrow."

"Ok then.".

When I get there Trill is over. "Shawty Red."

"Where you been I ain't been seeing you around. You know you rarely kick it with us anyway."

"I went to the A for a little bit."

"Oh, I was wondering. I thought 12 got you." I sit next to him.

"Hell no." He laughs. "I was out here getting it. You know me."

"Yeah, when you get your ass in trouble, you are going to want to stop."

"Nah." He picks up a cup and drink from it.

"Where you was last night? I was about to come looking for you when you didn't answer your phone."

"I was good. I had a great time last night."

"With who?" Trill questioned.

"Why you need to know?" I look at him.

"Cause I asked."

"Well, if yall must know I was out with Frank."

"Bartender Frank?"

"Yes, bartender Frank." I say with attitude.

"I thought you was fucking with buddy."

"He cool though. I went out with him. We kicked at his spot, that's it."

Being the type that Trill is, he keeps going with the questions. "What you mean by yall kicked it?"

"Are you my dude Trill." I laugh and he shaked his head no. "So, why you worried what kicked it mean."

"You fucked ole buddy and ain't give me none?"

"Fuck you Trill."

"You wild Trill." Aaron laughed, wiping his face with his hands.

"I'm about to go to the room. I'll see you in the morning." I leave and go to the room and lay down. All I thought about was what happened the night and morning before, and what I what tomorrow had in store for me.

Chapter 5

When I got out of the shower, I put on a cute red dress and some black heels. I had ten minutes before Frank was supposed to get here. I did my hair in some big curls going to the back with a deep side part.

"Going all out huh?" Aaron comes to the bathroom door. "You look good though sis."

"Thank you." I finish up my hair. "My Auntie told me about how my dad has money saved up for me in the bank, but I don't know how much it is. So, I'm going to use some of it to get a new place. And I was wondering can you help me look for one sometime next week when I'm off?"

"Yeah."

The doorbell rings.

"I'll get it," Aaron says.

"If its Frank, tell him I'll be out in a minute."

Aaron leaves out and answers the door. I spray on some perfume and put on some lip stick. I grab my purse and cell phone, and go into the living room where Frank is waiting.

"Hey."

"You ready?" he asks.

"Yeah." He gets up and we go to the door. "I'll be back later Aaron."

We get into his car and pull off from Aaron's apartment.

"How your day been?"

"It's been going good."

"Yeah. I been waiting all day to go out with you."

"I've been anxious to see you. I enjoyed the time we spent together."

"I did too." he said before pausing briefly, "You look so sexy tonight."

"Thank you. You are looking good too. Collared shirt, creased up, extra clean. I ain't mad at you." I smile.

"Yeah."

"So this restaurant must be very nice." I looked at him.

"They have the best food. You'll see when we get there."

When we get to the restaurant, the waitress takes us to our seats. Frank had called and made reservations for us, so it was easy getting a seat in this very full restaurant. We took a seat and later ordered our food, and starting conversation.

"Can I ask you a few questions to get know you a little better?"

"Yeah," he says after he finishes taking a sip of his drink. .

"Do you have any kids?"

"I have two boys and three girls."

"Are you serious?" I ask in disbelief.

"No, I was just kidding with you," He laughs.

"Oh, 'cause I was about to say damn." I drink some of my water. "Well, how are you with your family?"

"My mom and dad, we are good. I grew up living in Brooklyn."

"Where are they now?"

"My mom stays on the eastside and my pops stay in Brooklyn. After they divorced I moved down here with my mom, and then after a while I moved with dad. Then when I got older I moved back here."

"So, do you have any brothers and sisters?"

"I have two brothers. My brother next to me stays in Brooklyn. The youngest one is dead. He was murdered."

"Oh. I'm sorry to hear about that."

He had also experienced lost as I did, but I know he doesn't know what's it's like to lose three of the people that meant everything to you in life.

"It has been like six years now." He shrugs his shoulders.

I shake my head.

When we finished our meal, we go over to his to talk a while.

"I enjoyed myself tonight again," I smile at him.

"I'm glad you did." He picks up my hand and holds it. "Is there something that you just don't like at all?"

"I don't like people who lie. I rather know the hold true, then to find out later about it, because by then it probably can ruin everything."

"Well there is something that I should. I don't know how you are going to feel about this, but you need to know."

"What?" I ask curiously.

"I'm in the game."

"What you mean?" I ask puzzled as I turn to him.

"I'm a drug dealer."

I pause and say nothing.

"You alright."

I sit up in the seat and pull my hand away from him.

"Yeah, it's just... It's just my dad... He was a drug dealer. He was so deep in the game. My life was so perfect when he was around. I had everything that I wanted. Me and my mom was happy, and always getting along, but the day he was murdered changed my life for the worst. He was just coming back from being out on the streets, when he was walking in the house, two dudes came behind him and shot him walking up to the steps of the house. I was upstairs in my room and my mom was in the kitchen when it happened. After that my mom started drinking to hide her pain, but that didn't help. It only made the situation bad. And if I'm going to be with you, I don't want to have to go through nothing like that. That shit ran her straight through the ground and I can't put myself through the same thing."

"I'm sorry to hear that, but with me I stay low key, because I don't want anybody to know when I move. In these streets they know the name I go by, but they never seen the face.

The only people that know who I am, is my cousins Stretch and Boobie, then my homie I came up with. Any of the other soldiers go through them."

"Just because they are the only ones who know, doesn't mean somebody else can't find out. Losing my dad, my mom, and my boyfriend to death, I don't want to go down that road again."

"I can promise you that nothing is going to happen like that. Can you believe me?"

I look and see that he was being sincere. I hoped everything would be okay.

"I hope so, because I really like you."

"I like you too, so I don't want to make you hurt in any way, so you can't tell anyone."

"I won't."

He takes my hand again and kisses it all the way up my arm, until he reaches my mouth and we start kissing.

"Do you have to go to work tomorrow?"

"Yeah, I got to go in at eight."

"What time you get off?"

"At four."

"I might come through to see you at work, if I'm not busy handling business."

"My feet are hurting from them shoes."

"Let me massage them then." He moves to the other end of the couch and starts massaging my feet.

"You have some nice feet."

"Yeah. I keep them well pedicured."

"I like women who keep their hands and feet looking nice."

"Do you have some kind of fetish?"

"No I wouldn't call it a fetish."

"So you do you like to suck toes?"

He didn't answer, but he made clear when he licked the sole of my foot and started sucking on my toes. "I've been told that my tongue can work magic."

"That it does." I moan.

He takes my other foot and massages it.

"You like freaky stuff don't you."

"Yes if it's being done right. The only way I can be super freaky with a dude, is that he got to be able to deserve it. You just can't be randomly freaking people."

"Yeah. That's true." He starts rubbing on my thigh while he is still sucking and massaging my feet.

"That feels good, but come here."

Frank comes back up to me and I pull him to me and I start kissing on him. We get a lot of touchy feely, and I could feel him getting hard.

"You know I got to go to work tomorrow." I look at my cell phone. "NaNa done called me and it's late, so I mind as well be getting home."

"You sure you can't stay a little while longer or just let me take you to work in the morning."

"If I stay the night here I know I won't be getting any sleep and won't be up for work on time."

"Yeah." He wipes his lips off with his hand and stands up.

"I'm about to call NaNa back real quick."

"Alright, I'm about to go to the bathroom before we go."

"Ok." I call back NaNa to see what she wanted. "Yes, I saw that you called."

"You home?"

"Not yet. I'm at Frank's house right now. We are about to leave though."

"Yall must be had a great night."

"Shut up. No. I mean not in the way that you talking about. We have just been chillin."

"That's what you say."

"You don't have to believe me."

"We'll just call me when you get back."

"Ok."

"Bye."

I hang up the phone and Frank comes back from the bathroom. "You ready?"

"Yeah." I put back on my shoes, and pick up my purse from off the coffee table.

On the ride back, we listen to some slow music, enjoying the mood. When we get there, he gives me a good night kiss and I go inside. Aaron had already gone to bed. After I go to the room take off my shoes and take a shower I call NaNa back.

"I'm home." I sit down on the bed.

"So, what happened?"

"We went to a restaurant over there where he lives at, I don't remember the name, but they got some good ass food. After that, we went back to his place and talked some more. I was asking him a lot more question."

"Mhm."

" My feet was hurting so said that he would massage my feet for me. He kept talking about how I had such pretty feet and that he likes women with pretty hands and feet. I asked him did he suck toes. He didn't answer, but he showed me."

"So, he sucked your toes?"

"Yeah, and it felt good girl." I lay down on the bed.

"You are getting excited about that. This tells me that you really haven't been in a relationship in a long time and ain't been hit by a freak either."

"Anyway I stopped him, and I started kissing him and he was so ready, but I knew if I was to stay any longer I wouldn't of made it to work on time."

"Forget work. If my baby ret-to-go, believes we doing something."

I laugh. "But you know me. I need my rest to get up on time. Next time I'm not holding out. It was a major stress release when we was together the other day."

"That's why you hardly ever see me angry."

"I know."

"Your other boo ain't call you today?" she pops her tongue.

"Jeremy?"

"Who else?"

"No. His girl must have been around all day. I swear he have too much free time to talk to me. If I was her, my man would never have the time to worry about entertaining someone else. He says that the don't get to spend much time together."

"She is slacking on something good."

"Yeah. You know, it's one thing that I never told you before?"

"What? I thought we would never keep secrets from one another."

I sit up. "Well, you know how after prom, I told you I didn't feel good and I wasn't going to the party, and that Jeremy didn't want to go without me?"

"Yeah."

"Well, it really didn't go down like that. Me and Jeremy had hooked up after prom."

"Oh my god, you lying," she says excited.

"For real."

"Why you never told me about it?"

"Because, we wanted no one but us to know about it, and that's why I shouldn't even be telling you now."

"But you know you got to tell me what all happened."

"No. That's for me and him to only know, well and the people next door in the hotel room to know." I laugh.

"Damn. He was putting it down like that?"

"Yes. That's why I'm wondering what's his girl problem is. Well now I see why she the way she is."

"For real."

"But, let me get some sleep, so I can get up."

"Call me tomorrow."

"I will. Bye." I end the call and lay my phone on the night stand, then drift off to sleep with Frank on my mind.

Chapter 6

The next morning, I woke up at about seven to get ready for work. When I got there, it was the same old thing. I worked the register at Shoe Infinity. My friend who we call Miami worked there with me. We met through working here and became real cool.

"I'm ready for my break."

"Me too." I reply. "It seem like the day is going by so slow."

"Tell me about it."

Things were moving kind of slow today and when it was slow, time seemed to slow down as well.

"I know last we was talking about your boo Marc. Did he ever get the job?"

"Yeah, he started today, and I'm glad. All he did was sit around all day doing nothing but look after

Landon, watch TV, and ate up all the food that I paid for all by myself. I told him my mama ain't raised no fool."

"I know that's right."

"I may be younger than him, but I ain't no dummy. If you can't pull your share in, I can't do it for you. I don't have time trying to take care of a grown ass man when it's hard enough taking care of my little boy. The only reason we still together is because of Landen, but I know it ain't going to last too much longer if he don't start making some changes in his life."

I nod my head.

"I got mama watching him now while we both at work. I know she going to start tripping if she have to watch him all the time, so I'm going to have put him in daycare pretty soon."

A customer came up to my register smiling extra hard.

"Will this be all?"

"Yeah. What's your name beautiful?"

I pull my tag to show him. "Read."

"Yolanda huh?"

I tell him his total and he pays for it, but still didn't move away from the counter.

"That's a pretty name to match that sexy face."

"Thank you." He was starting to get on my nerves already.

"Shawty, you got a man?"

"Yes I do," I put my hand on my hips.

"Well, I ain't trying to be nothing but a friend."

"Ok, well friend can you move out of line so I can get the rest of my customers?"

He turns around and sees people behind him. "Oh my bad." He moves out of the way, but is still there.

I check out one of the two people that was in line, then he comes back.

"Can I get your number, so I can call you sometime?"

"Yeah." I write down a fake number and give it to him, because I was ready from him to get out of my face.

"Alright. I'll catch you some other time."

"Bye." I roll my eyes as he walks away.

"So desperate," Miami says.

"I know right. Dude thought he was going to get my real number. Man please."

"But, you always seem to pull 'em all in."

"The majority of them ain't even worth it. I hate when people run up on me like that."

"Give me the attention. I would love it."

Break comes around and I go to the food court to get something to eat. While I'm sitting out there Frank walks up.

"Hey baby," Frank greets me with a hug.

"Hey."

"I figured you were on break, so I came to stop by." He takes a seat at the table with me.

"What you been up to today?" I look up at him.

"Just been handling some business."

"Oh ok."

"I was going by my mom house this afternoon, and I wanted to know if you wanted to ride?"

"Yeah, I'll go with you. What time you going?"

"At seven."

"Oh ok. I get off at four. You can just come by Aaron's and pick me up."

"Ok."

"You want some?"

"Yeah, I'll get some." He takes my plate and eats some of my food.

"I can't wait to get off either. I want to go and relax a little."

"I know what you mean." He puts the fork down in the container.

"Can you cook?"

"What?"

"Can you cook? I see you have a big kitchen and you look like a man that knows his way in a kitchen."

"Yeah I do. My mom taught me. Why you asked that out the blue?"

"I don't know. I just wanted to know."

"Can you cook?"

"To survive yeah, but I can't cook a big meal."

"Well, I'm going to have to teach you." He looks at me.

"Ok. I'll take you up on that." I smile.

We talk some more, then I have to get back to work. At four I get off work and head back to Aaron's so I could get ready to go with him to his mother's house. On my way back to the house Jeremy calls.

"Hey Jey."

"What up?"

"I just got off now I'm headed home. Then I got to get ready, because I'm riding with my friend to his mom house with him."

70

"Oh, so he got you meeting mama already?"

"I guess so. What you up to?"

"I'm just leaving the library right now, headed back to the apartment."

"See, that's what I want to be able to do. Go to school so I can get me a better job than working at the mall."

"You can."

"But I got to get myself together first. I'm trying to get me a place. My dad got me money saved up, but I got to see what that's looking like."

"Yeah, but you should try college though. I know you smart, and you use to like school, so I know you'll like it."

"Yeah. I want to do that." I pull up to a stop light. "You must was busy yesterday?"

"Yeah, you can say that." He laughs.

"Mm. I hope she know what she doing, because you can't waste nothing like that." I laugh.

"Barely though."

"That's not good," I joke.

"I know right."

"I know you ready for spring break."

"Hell yeah. I plan on coming back down there."

The light changes. "Ok. We might have to go party or something. Are you bringing your girl?"

"Nah, she going to spend time with her family."

"Oh. You know I finally told NaNa why we really didn't go to the after party after prom."

"Oh for real."

"I didn't go into details though. I told her that was just for me and you to know."

"I still ain't tell nobody. As much as I wanted to, I didn't."

"That's the only thing I ever kept from her too."

"How long yall two been friends?"

"Since the third grade when she moved up here. We always had each other back on everything."

"Yeah. Where you at right now?"

"I'm two blocks away from Aaron's house." I beep the horn. "These damn people need to watch where they going. Lady trying to back up right in the street."

"Don't get hurt."

"I'm not, but if she kept backing up, she would have been if she had hit my car, because I would of got out and whipped her ass."

"Girl you crazy," he laughs.

"Tell me something I don't know." I pull in to the apartments that Aaron stay at, and park my car. I get out and go in the house. "I'm here now."

"Alright. I'm about to go get me something to eat."

"Okay then. Just call me back when you get finish."

"Ok."

"Alright." I hang up with him. "Hey Aaron. Hello."

"What up? This is my friend Fallon." Aaron introduces his lady friend.

"Hey, you must be Yolanda?"

"Yeah that's me. Aaron, I'm to be gone again tonight. I'll call you if I come back."

"Alright."

I go into the room and take a shower, and then get dressed. After a while Jeremy calls me back and we talk some more, before he made his way back to his house. When we get off the phone Frank picked me up and we were on our way to his mom house on the eastside.

"You think she's going to like me?"

"Yeah my mom is a nice lady. I'm going to tell you right now, she's going to try to feed you when we get there. She always does that to anyone who comes over."

"Ok. I'm hungry anyways." I rub my stomach.

"How has your day been?" he asks.

"The first half of work was boring until you came. Then I was straight since then."

He picks my hand up from the center console and holds my hand. "You know I really like you Yolanda? I really feel that you fit me."

"I like you too. If I didn't, I wouldn't have ever been with you."

"I've seen you turn down a lot of guys before."

"I really wasn't looking to get in a relationship or anything really. Ever since Ace was killed, I never connected with anyone, and the one person I did let in he wasn't on his game like should have been."

"A girl like you needs a real man that knows what to do with you."

"And you that man?"

"Hell yeah, and you know it."

I giggle. "Yeah, we will see."

Soon we get to his mom's house. We pull up in her drive way, and she comes to the car.

"Hey Frankie baby." She comes to the driver side of the car.

"Hey ma." He says as he gets out. "This is my girlfriend Yolanda."

"Hey how you doing?"

I get out the car and go to where they are standing. "Hey, I'm doing good."

"You're just as pretty as my Frankie said."

I smile. "Thank you."

"Yall come on in."

Frank turns to me and whispers in my ear as him mom steps up on the porch. "I told you she was nice."

"Yeah."

When we go in the house, it's a little boy and little girl running around in the house.

"Yall stop that running," his mom says.

"That is my nephew Tahji and niece Aaliyah."

"Your brother's kids?"

"Yeah."

"Uncle Frank." Tahji runs up to Frank with a hug, and Aaliyah follows.

"Hey. This is my girlfriend Yolanda."

"Yall can call me Applez."

"Applez. I love apples. Do you like apples?" Aaliyah asks.

"Yeah I do." I laugh.

"I like apples too." Tahji seconds. "The green one's are the best."

"No the red ones are." Aaliyah disagrees.

"Yes they are."

They begin to argue.

"Hey, hey. Both are good. Now don't argue about it." Frank changed subjects by asking what happened at school.

"We went on a field trip today to the Okefenokee Swamp." Aaliyah says.

"We had a play in our class today on the Wizard of Oz."

"Ok." Frank replies as he sits down on the arm of the chair.

"What grade are yall in?" I ask.

"I'm in the second grade and Aaliyah is in the third grade."

"Oh ok. Yall are so cute." I sit next to Frank.

"Thank you," Aaliyah smiles.

Frank's mom went into the kitchen. It smelt like she was cooking some fried chicken and tomatoes and rice.

"It smells good in here."

"Fried chicken."

"What is your mom's name?"

"Danielle, but everybody call her Mama D."

I nod my head.

"Mama D comes back in the living room with a fork in her hand. "Yall can wash up and come to eat."

"You must have known that she was going to cook?" I ask.

"Yeah. Actually I called her and told her to cook for us."

I hit Frank on the leg as he gets up to go to the bathroom to wash his hands, and I follow him. It was a nice house.

"I like this house."

"I bought it for her."

"Oh, I like it. I need to start looking for me a place like Wednesday."

"I can help you if you want me too." He dries his hand on a towel.

"I asked Aaron to help, but you can help instead. I know Aaron might have something to do."

I dry my hands off and we go into the kitchen. Tahji and Aaliyah are already at the table, and Mama D is fixing plates for us.

I sit down at the table on the other side of Tahji and Frank sits in the chair next to me.

Mama D places our plates in front of us, then she sits down, and she tells Frank to say grace, and we begin to eat. After we finished, we talked some.

"Frank has been speaking mighty highly of you Ms. Yolanda. He says that you are a good girl."

"Thank you Frank." I smile and grab his arm. "The food was great. I haven't had a real home cooked meal in a long time."

"Well, you need to come by more often."

"I will."

"Grandma, can we go back in the living room and play?" Tahji asks.

"Yeah, yall can go."

They get up from the table and run to the living room.

"I'm sorry to hear about what happened to your parents."

I nod my head.

"I was watching the news that night when your mom was in the wreck."

76

"Losing both of my parents was very hard on me."

"Trust me baby I know. But what hurt most was having to bury my baby boy." I could see that Frank's mom was starting to get emotional about speaking about her son.

"Ma, I'll wash dishes for you."

"I'll help him."

"Thank you baby. I'm about to go in here and try to watch some TV while these children in here playing."

"Ok."

Me and Frank get up and go to the sink to wash the dishes.

"I purposely made sure it was a dish washer in this house so she wouldn't have to wash dishes by hand, but she insists on doing them herself. She claims that it doesn't wash the dishes good enough."

"That's how my mom was."

We wash the dishes and go into the living room with Mama D and talk and everything, then later we leave and head back to his place, but on the way he ask me do I want to spend a night. We are on our way to Aaron's house so I can get me some clothes to leave in the morning.

"I better call him before we go over."

I call Aaron, but he doesn't answer his phone. I knew what was going on.

"He ain't picking up?"

"No. I don't want to disturb him when we get there."

We go to Aaron's place and I get out and go to the door and unlock it. When you get in, all you can hear moans and screaming.

"Damn Aaron." I said as I went to my room and packed a bag real quick.

"Yeah right there, yeah baby. Work this pussy like you own it," you could hear the girl scream.

I leave out of the apartment laughing

"What's so funny?" Frank asks.

"Sounds like a porno going on in there for real." We both laugh.

"You got to go to work tomorrow?"

"Yeah, you going to take me?"

"Yeah. I will."

We go back to his place. When we get there, we go up to his room and lay at the foot of his bed and watch TV, and talk.

"Thank you for taking me to your mom's house. I had a good time meeting her and you nephew and niece."

"I knew you would, besides I wanted my mom to meet the woman that I'm falling for."

"You really falling for me?"

"I am and it's crazy, because I've never felt like this for someone so fast. Ever." He leans over to me and kisses me. "I know we haven't been together long, but I just know you are the one for me."

I pull him to me and we start kissing. He pulls my shirt up and over my head, and starts kissing on my navel and up to my breast. My phone rings, I look at it and ignored it, it was NaNa. He pulls my titties out of the bra and start sucking on them. He lets his hands

78

explore the rest of my body. My phone rings again so I answer.

"Yeah." I say in a distressed voice.

"What you doing?"

Frank makes his way with his hand into my pants, and starts having a field day.

"Ooo I'll ca...call you back later," I moan and hang up the phone.

He unbuttons my pants and pulls them off of me. He comes back up my body and sucks on my hard nipples as he slips a finger inside of me and starts to twirl his finger around. He slowly makes his way back down my body and spreads my legs wide and pushes them to me and licks my pussy so good.

"I love you," Frank says.

"I love," I moan, "you too."

He goes back to eating and I loved every moment of it. I lift his head up and I tell him to lay down. When he does I climb on top of him and slowly sliding down on his fully erect dick until it was all the way inside, which was hard to do. I place my hands down over his shoulder and move up and down slowly on him.

I tighten up my pussy muscles around him. "You like that baby?"

"Yeah," he groans. He rubs his hands up my body.

I sit up and grind on him. He takes my hands and I hold his hands as I'm grinding hard.

"Ride my shit," Frank insists.

I start bouncing up and down on him, grinding my hips. He starts bouncing me up. After he makes me get mine, he gets on top of me and holds my legs straight up in the air, so that he could hit every spot.

"Right there baby." He was making my whole body quivers. Tears start falling from my face it was so good.

A while later, I could feel him reaching his peak, before he came he pulled out and came on my stomach. I forgot he didn't put on a condom. He grabbed the towel that was sitting on the head of the bed and whipped me off. He leans over and gives me a kiss.

I get up and go to the bathroom to take a shower, and Frank decided to join me. It quickly turned into round two when he started kissing on my neck, this time he had a condom in his hand. We were back at it again. After that round, we washed and got in bed and went to sleep.

Chapter 7

Frank was still asleep when I woke up. I went to the bathroom and got ready for my day at work. After I put my clothes on, I went back over to the bed to wake him up.

"Baby wake up so you can take me to work." I shake him.

"I'm getting up." He sits up in the bed and wipes his eyes. "You ready already?"

"Yeah. I got to be there at ten."

"Alright. After I put on my clothes I'll be ready."

When he goes to the bathroom, I go downstairs to wait on him. Ten minutes later he comes down.

"Ok I'm ready."

I get my purse and we go outside to the car and we leave for me to go to work.

"Thank you."

"No, thank you," he replies.

I give him a good bye kiss.

"Remember I get off work at 5:00 so be here."

I get out and go inside to work.

It was definitely a great day, because I was on a high from Frank. It felt good to be in a relationship with someone and developing very strong feeling for that person. I hadn't felt this feeling in a very long while, and it was very pleasing.

Work was going by very smoothly and my break was creeping up. A little bit before break NaNa stops by to pay me a little visit.

"Hey Applez."

"Hey NaNa."

"Um, we need to talk."

"Ok, my break is in like five minutes. I'll be out there in a minute."

"Yeah. I'll be over there getting a pizza."

"Ok."

In no time, I joined NaNa at the food court to talk and for something to eat.

"What was that all about last night? Sound like somebody was getting some things done."

Cracking a huge smile was all I could do. "You caught me at a good ass time. We was just getting it started."

"Damn girl."

"Yeah. But I did something I didn't think I'll ever do so quick, because I was so caught up in it all." I whispered in her ear. "He went in raw."

"No. I know you didn't let him..."

"Hell no, I ain't that stupid. I was so caught up in then moment that I forgot. After that though, I went to take a shower, and he came and got in with me. This time he was strap, and we got back to it."

"Mm."

"But you know what he told me."

"What?" she sits down her soda.

"He told me that he loved me, and I told him that I loved him back."

"Did you mean it?"

"I don't know. I really like him, but I don't know if I can call it love yet. He took me to his mama house earlier that day too."

"Well, we know he loves you, because he comfortable enough for you to meet moms, but yours will come in time though."

"Yeah." I take a slice of pizza.

We talk and eat until it's time for me to go back to work. When it was time to get off, I went outside and Frank was nowhere to be found. I called his phone, but got no answer.

"Where is he at?" I look down the street. "I'm going to call him one more time."

I call again and he doesn't answer. Now I have to call NaNa to come and get me. When she pulls up, I get in the car.

"You told him what time he was supposed to come get you?"

"Yeah I told him soon as I got out the car this morning that I get off at five. I don't know where he is at?"

"This ain't no good look."

"Not at all." I slip down in the seat some. "But I hope everything is all right with him." I was starting to get a little concerned.

On the way to her house, I saw a house I wanted to look at and we stopped and got the number. Hopefully this would be a place that I would be considering moving to.

When we got to her house Damien was home, which I rarely ever seen him there this time of day.

"Hey Damien. I ain't seen you in a good little minute."

"I know. Been out doing me. You know, same old thing."

"Yeah."

"Hey baby," NaNa gives him a kiss.

My phone rings and it's Frank.

"Hello."

"I'm sorry baby. I lost track of time, I was handling a little business with my cousin," he tries to apologize.

"Yeah. I had to call NaNa to pick me up."

"Is it anything I can do to make it up you?"

With him already knowing what time I got off and saying he would be there to pick me up, I would think he would have kept track of his time. "No you good."

"You want me to pick you up from over there?"

"No. I'm going to get NaNa to take me over to Aaron's house. I'm staying there tonight and get some rest."

"Ok."

"Can you call me back later though?" I sit down on the porch.

"Yeah, I'll talk to you later."

"Bye." I end the call, shaking my head.

I go back inside and tell NaNa to take me home. When I get back, I unlock the door and go inside. Aaron was just coming from out of the back.

"What's up?"

"Oh nothing much," I sit down and take off my shoes. "Oh, yesterday I came back by to get some clothes and I heard you tearing ole girl down in there."

Aaron starts laughing. "Man I'm tryna tell ya."

"I was like bru must be slanging good wood got her hollering like that."

"If they ain't know, now they do." We both laugh.

I pick up the remote and turn on the TV.

"What you been up to yesterday?" Aaron sits down.

"I went to Frank's mom's house and had dinner with her and his nephew and niece."

He shook his head.

"Do you know he didn't come by to pick me up after work, and I had to get NaNa to come get me?"

"He ain't call you?"

"After I was already at NaNa's house. I was sitting out there for a good thirty minutes, and you know when I get off work I'm ready to come home. He asked me did I want to come over tonight, but after that little stunt, I'm fine with where I'm at."

"I know."

"Are you still going to come with me to help me find a place? I saw this one house on the way to NaNa's house from work. It looked nice on the outside. I wrote down the information from the for sale sign." I turn the TV to the movie stations to try and find something to watch.

"I got to work tomorrow. We can go another time though."

"I really wanted to go tomorrow since I'm off. I did tell Frank if something came up I would ask him to come with me. I guess I'll call him and let him know. Oh yeah, when I get paid Friday, I'll pay you for the time I've been staying here, because I don't want to seem like a free loader or anything."

"You know that's cool Applez. You don't have to pay me anything."

"You sure, because when I leave I don't want you to be like well damn sis came thru and ain't even try to pay me nothing."

"You know I ain't like that."

"Yeah. I need to call him back." I get up and go to the room and give Aaron the remote.

I sit down on the bed and call up Frank.

"What up baby?" he answers.

"You remember when I told you if Aaron wasn't going to be able to come with me to look for a place, I wanted you to come?"

"Yeah."

"Well, he got to work tomorrow and I want you to come with me, that is if when I call these people they say I come by the house and look at it."

"Alright. I am sorry about earlier."

"I told you I was cool about it. Even though I was standing out there for waiting, I'm okay. NaNa came and got me. I'm straight."

"After you call about the house call me back and let me know."

"Oh, I will. Talk to you later."

"Alright bye."

"Bye." I end the call and take out the number out of my pocket to call the people who owned the house.

"Hello."

"Hey, is this Jonathan Michaels?"

"Yes."

"I'm calling about a house that I saw that I would like to come and see."

"Oh. You're talking about the crème colored house on 36th and Anderson.

"Yes sir. Will I be able to come see it tomorrow?"

"Yes. Could you come by at one to view it?"

"That will be good for me."

"Then at one it will be. Do you have any questions for me now?"

"Is it a two bedroom house?"

"Yes with a master bathroom inside of the master bedroom. The other bathroom will be in the hall."

"Ok. I'll be over tomorrow at one to see it."

"See you then."

I hang up the phone and call Frank back. This time I told him I'll pick him up so he can come with me to see it. I was going to have to go by the bank to check on my account and the one my dad had for me. I was feeling bored, so I decided to text Jeremy.

I tell him about how I'm looking for a house, and he tells me how he is coming down here for the weekend. We plan on going out together when he does come.

The rest of the night I stayed home and chill.

This morning I called Frank to make sure he was up. I let him know that I was on my way. Since I was up early I went by the bank to check out my accounts. When I go, I find out that my dad had a lot of money in there. Most of it I know was for college, but it still was enough to get a place. I was so happy.

When I got there I go up to the door and knock. He comes to the door and greets me with a hug and kiss.

"Hey," I say as he releases his arms from around me.

"I missed seeing you yesterday." We walk into his house.

"Yeah. I would have come, but I was tired."

"I washed your clothes that you left when I washed mine yesterday."

"Thank you baby. I was going to wash them this weekend when I wash all my clothes. So you ready to go?" I ask.

"Yeah I am." He puts his keys in his pocket and we walk to the door and he opens it for me.

"Are you going to be busy tonight, because I wanted to come over?"

"No, I'm free." He locks the door behind him, and we get in the car.

"After we get finish I'll stop by and get me some clothes to wear tomorrow."

"You must don't have to go to work tomorrow."

"Yeah I do, but this time I got my car," I joke with him. I pull out of the driveway and head over to the house.

When we get the owner of the house, Jonathan Michaels was standing outside.

"Hello my name is Yolanda Smith. I'm the one who called you yesterday about the house."

"Ok, I'm Jonathan, and this is my wife Amanda."

"Hello," Amanda greets us with a hand shake.

"Will you both be wanting to live at this residence?"

"No. He's just helping me out."

"Ok. Yall can come inside."

We go inside the house and look at everything. The house came with a new washer and dryer. I planned on getting me a whole new living room and bedroom suit. I planned on putting the furniture in my mom's house in storage or just sell it all together. I would worry about getting a bed for the guest room later. If I were to be approved for the house I would be happy. Frank and I thought that the house was very good and the price was good for the great condition the house was in.

After we get through with that, I stop by Aaron's house to get some clothes to wear since I was spending the night at Frank's house. We went back to his place and chilled and watched some movies and went to sleep.

The next day I wake up early and Frank is up cooking breakfast.

"Good morning," he says as he puts my food in front of me.

"Good Morning. Thank you." I sit down on the stool around the island. "I hope it taste as good as it smells."

"If you liked my mom food, I know you going to like mine." He sits down across from me.

I eat some of the food he cooked and it did taste good. "Are you going to cook me something for when I get off?"

"Are you coming to stay the night again?"

"Yeah, if you let me."

"You know you can baby." He starts eating.

When I get finish eating, I get up and wash my dish. Frank walks me to the door and gives me a kiss and grabs my booty.

"Aye now."

"See ya later," he says as I walk to my car and open the door.

"Ok," I close the door, crank up and drive off.

When I got off from work I called Frank before going over. We went out to the movies and came back home and fall asleep in the living room.

On a Friday afternoon, I get a call from Jeremy saying that he was coming to town and we plan to go out. I personally didn't want to go to my usual spot because Frank was working that night. I told Frank that I would be hanging out with a friend, so I might not come thru.

"Hey Jey." I answer the phone.

"Yeah, I'm back," he says as he clears his throat.

"Where are you at, because I hear kids?"

"I'm at my cousin Trey house. You hear his sons running around playing."

"Oh ok."

"So what are you doing?"

"I'm just at Aaron's ready to get out of the house and do something."

"I'll be over there in a little bit and we can figure out what we are going to do when I get there."

"Ok."

"I'll be there in a minute."

Jeremy hangs up and I go put on something cute to go out in. I wasn't to sure of what we would do, but anything was better than sitting around being bored.

When Jeremy made it, we decided to go bowling. I hadn't been bowling in a while, so I knew that it would be fun. On the way there, we talked.

"I told my boyfriend I was going out with a friend today so it's cool."

"Who is ole buddy anyways?"

"You know Frank that work the bar at the club that I go too all the time?"

"Yeah."

"Him."

"How yall get together?"

"Frank has liked me for a good while now, but the only reason I never wanted to talk to him was because he's older than me."

"You know I like you, but why you don't want to get with me?"

"You have a girlfriend Jeremy." I turn to him.

"What about before that? Before me and her was together."

"You know after Ace died I went through my little phase. I swore I wouldn't date anybody until I found that one who was just as good as him, but I had to learn I was being unrealistic."

"I wish that you could see how good I am."

"We go through this all the time Jey. Yeah I like you, but ..."

"But what? I felt it and you felt it, that day I left when I gave you that kiss."

I say nothing but directed my attention in front of me, because I didn't want Jeremy to read how I felt on my face. I haven't felt what I feel with him since prom night. Yes, I was really feeling Frank, but it was a different feeling. But how can I be going through something like this now that I'm with somebody?

When we get to the bowling alley, we park in front of the building. We get out get our shoes and stuff and go bowl. We have lots of fun. He started winning, but my score was right behind his.

"Watch I pass you. You trying to showing off now. Aye, you remember when we went on that field trip in middle school and afterwards we went bowling."

"Yeah and Jalissa fell and busted her ass." We started laughing.

"That day was too funny. Dank got caught kissing Nita and they got in trouble." I lay over on Jeremy laughing.

"Yeah, those were the good days back then."

"What we doing after we eat?"

"I don't know if you down with it, but you want to go to the strip club?"

"Yeah I guess so. It shouldn't be a problem, as long as they keep they ass out of my face, because I don't get down like that. Not at all." I shake my head.

"You are a cool ass girl for real, because I know some girl act like they too good to go.

We finish up bowling and Jeremy wins by a few points. After we get something to eat we leave from there and go straight to the strip club.

We pull up to a place called Playas Delight. A girl and a guy were coming out, she looked like a dancer, and you know what they were getting ready to do.

It was real live in there when we walked in. On the right side of us it was this dude getting a table dance with a girl half naked and on the other side a girl had her ass tooted up in this guy's face and he was smacking it. On stage was two girl working it to some shit I had never heard before and they was getting a lot of money tossed up to them and put in their garter belts.

"You like that right there huh? Yeah I see you," Another girl tells this dude she was giving a lap dance to as we passed them.

Me and Jeremy go to the bar and get a drink before we sit down to loosen up a little. We sat down at a table close to the stage. It was dudes surrounding the stage as this girl they announce called Jamaican Dyme comes out in a Jamaican colored outfit, with some of the same colors in her dreads.

I take a sip of my drink. "They live in here huh?" I ask Jeremy.

"Yeah."

A girl comes over to us and she was very pretty. She looked like she could be doing a lot more than being in here dancing for her money. She had some pretty grey eyes. "Do you want a dance sexy." Jeremy says yeah and she starts dancing on him.

Another girl comes over and you could tell she was into female. She had a tongue ring and her lip pierced. She came straight to me.

"Damn baby girl you are fine as hell. You want a dance?"

"No thank you. I'm just here with my friend."

"Too bad." She comes behind me and whispers in my ear. "I can make you like it." She rubs her hand up my arm. "Let me get a taste of that kitty and you'll see."

"No. I'm strictly dick home girl, please back up off me."

She moves from behind me and leave. I look to Jeremy and he was enjoying his dance. She had her top off now, and she told Jeremy to feel on her tits, and he did so. She then turned around and sat in his lap and started grinding. I could tell how her facial expression changed that she felt what I once had for a night. Jeremy dropped her a few bills into her garter on her leg and on her arm. I saw as the girl took Jeremy's hand

and was about to place it in her panties, but I pulled it away.

"This your girl?" She keeps grinding.

"No. I'm his friend." I was pretty jealous of the hold thing really. "I'll be right back." I get up and go to the bar.

The bartender was also a woman. I ordered my drink and she quickly makes it and I return to my seat.

"You good." Jeremy asks.

"Yeah I'm good."

It gets really live in there, and even I get up and start dancing on Jeremy for fun and dudes was asking me for a dance, but I was like I don't even work here. After I had another drink and that contact smoke, I was having a good time. We left at almost one.

When we get to Aaron's house me and Jeremy sits in the car and talk. He leans in to me and gives me a kiss. I didn't resist and kissed him back, and he out his hand around the back of my neck. His tongue slowly starts easing into my mouth. Then I thought about it and a picture of Frank popped up into my mind.

"I got to go. I'll talk to you later." I open the door and walk down to Aaron's apartment and Jeremy leaves. I knew I couldn't keep doing this with him. Before I go inside I call Frank.

"Hey baby you at the club still?"

"Yeah. You coming through?"

"If you want me to."

"Yeah I want you to come to my house tonight too."

"Ok. I'll come, I'll be there in a little bit."

"Alright. It's some people at the bar, so I'll get at you when you get here."

"Alright." I end the call and take my keys from my purse and go to the car and head to the club.

When I get there I go to where Frank is at.

"Hey baby." He leans from over the counter and give me a kiss.

"What's up? You want something to drink?"

"No, I'm good. I already had something tonight when I went out with my friend."

"Alright. You had a good time?"

"Yeah it was straight, we had fun and everything." I sit down.

"You're Team been here tonight."

"They love going out without me now."

A dude comes up behind me. "What up, you want to dance?"

I look at Frank and he nods his head yeah. "Yeah we can do that." I get up from the bar and they are playing one of my favorite songs and the club gets hype.

When we get to the dance floor we start dancing. I turn to face Frank and he is watching me as he is making someone a drink. I seductively dance while looking at him. He never took his eye of me as I danced to the song. After that song Rick Ross song "Money Make Me Cum" played. I don't remember the last time I heard that song, but everybody still loved it. I continued looking at my baby.

As me and the guy was dancing, he starts talking into my ear. "I can give you something to make you cum." He pulls my hair over my shoulder. "I know you feel that what you grinding on."

"Yeah, but I got a man."

"He ain't got to know," he kisses on my neck.

"But he already knows."

"How?"

"You see the guy working at the bar looking this way?"

"Yeah."

"That's my boyfriend." I move his hand from off of my waist and walk over to Frank.

"What was he saying?" he says as soon as I get over.

"Talking some ole bull shit. What time you get off?"

"I can ask Dennis to cover for me for the rest of the night."

"Do that, because..." I pull him down to me and whisper in his ear. Then I push him back up and he is smiling.

"Alright hold on." He goes over and talks Dennis into working the bar for him. When he comes back we leave and go back to his place.

When we get there he totes me upstairs to his bedroom and laid me down and pulls off my pants. He pulls up my shirt and start kissing on my stomach, and then his phone rings.

"Please don't answer that." I say pulling him back down to me. "We need you," I point to my lower half.

He looks at his caller ID. "I got to, it's my cousin." He gives me one quick kiss on the lips before he pick up the phone.

"What's up?" The hold conversation sounded real serious. I can tell that he was getting mad, because of his facial expression. "Alright I'll be there." He ends the call and stands up.

"What's wrong baby," I say as I sit up."

"Somebody stole a package of ours, and I got to go and see what's up?" he says as he buttons his shirt back up.

"You got to go right now?"

"Yeah, but I'll be back in a little bit." He gives me a kiss on the cheek, and walk out of the room.

"Damn!" I grunt in sexual desperation.

I hoped he came back soon, because I was feining for him at that moment. I could believe he has to go, but I was going to try to stay up and await his return.

After an hour or so of trying to stay, I couldn't take it anymore and fell asleep stretched out across his bed. A while later I get waked up by a kiss on the back of the neck.

"Hey. I tired staying up for you."

"It took longer than I expected. Come to find out it was one of my pons who stole the package, and he had to get dealt with."

"What you mean got dealt with?" I turn over and sat up.

"He had what was coming for him. When we rolled up on him he already knew what was coming for, so he shot at us and we got him before he hit us."

"You mean you killed him?"

He said nothing, but tried to kiss on me. "What's your problem?" I don't look him in the eyes. "Like I said he had what was coming for him. He messed up before and he had his ticket out when he shot at us."

He pulls my chin in his direction and kisses me on the lips, but I wasn't in the mood for it now.

"Come on, stop being all tense. I won't hurt you."

I lay down as he started kissing on me like nothing ever happened. He pulled off my panties and put on a condom and he slowly entered me. I know he could tell the way I was feeling, so he did all the work. It was almost six in the morning before we finished and he went to sleep right there. I stayed up for another thirty minutes just thinking about everything that was said and wondered what happened.

Chapter 8

The previous night had got to me and Frank could tell how I was acting the next day. I couldn't get it out of my mind that he had just killed someone.

"What's wrong with you? You can't still be trippin off of last night?"

I shake my head no. "I don't know. It's just...I don't know."

"Please don't do this shit. My last girl claimed she was down for me, but she wanted to pull out. You said you loved me and if that's so, you'll be down for whatever I do no matter the consequences. I told you nothing will happen to me, and I promise you that so I won't hurt you. Did you mean it when you said that you loved me?"

"Yeah." I shake my head.

"Alright then." He gives me a kiss on the forehead. "I'm about to go out."

"I'm about to leave too, I need to see what NaNa is up to." I get up and walk to the door, but it really felt like I was running.

"You ain't going to give me a kiss before you leave?"

Leaving his house, I knew I needed to talk with NaNa about this situation. She knew the life of a drug dealers girl, so she would be able to help me out.

"Hey girl, come on in." She says when she opens up the door. I follow her living room where we sat down.

"What you doing over here? I can't seem to keep up with you since you and Frank is always together."

"I have something to tell you, but you have to promise not to tell anybody. Especially not Aaron or Mieko, because I know they will trip."

"What is it?" She was concerned.

"I haven't told you, but Frank is a drug dealer. He told me not to tell anybody, but after what he did last night I knew I at least needed to talk to you about it. He killed somebody last night, and I can't get it off of my mind."

"Damn. I know I ain't the one to talk, but that do not sound good."

"Have you heard of someone they call Phantom in the streets?"

"Yeah. Is that really Frank." NaNa put one and two together.

I nod my head. "He's so lowkey with everything that no one knows that that is him. The only reason he told me was because in the beginning, I told him that I didn't want to get hurt by anything that he could hide from me, so he said he felt like he should tell me about it."

"At least he told you up front, but I don't understand why you would stay with him, after knowing that, when you were the one to say you will never be a drug dealer's girl."

"I know, I know, but I can't help the way that I feel for him. I really do like him and think I'm falling in love with him."

"Well, I can't make up your mind for you and since you say you love him, be ready to put up with what comes with dating someone like him."

I took into consideration what she was telling me. She was right, I always said I would never date anyone who was a drug dealer. Not knocking what my dad did, I didn't want to live that life and possibly end up like my mother.

"So, what did you and Jeremy do yesterday?"

"I picked me and we went out bowling, and I did something I never thought I would do."

"What, fuck him again?"

"No stupid." She laughs. "We went to Playas Delight."

"I wouldn't think you would do anything like that?"

"Me either, but we had a pretty good time. Jeremy had him a little lap dance, and home girl was getting a little too frisky. She was trying to put his hand down her panties, and I politely moved his hand before she could do it."

"Do I detect a little jealousy?"

"No. Anyways this girl came up to me, and she you can tell she was in to girls. She had a tongue ring, and a lip ring. Came over and talking about sexy let me get a dance and I was like no thank you, but that wasn't enough. Then she was like to bad, and she started rubbing on my arm and whispered in my ear talking about she can make me like it and let her taste my kitty and I'll see. I was like no baby girl I'm strictly dick."

"Hell naw."

"That's what I was like, but it was fun though. After I had a few more drinks I started dancing for Jeremy, and again the day ended with a kiss. This time I was into it too, but then a picture of Frank popped up in my head. I pushed him away from me and I was like I had to go and that I would talk to him later."

"Dang girl."

"It's like every time I get around him I feel different, but I don't want to keep going through this with him."

"I really don't know what to say about it, because I ain't never had to go through nothing like that, but just do what you feel is right. If you love Frank like you say stick with him, but if you like Jeremy..." she shrugs her shoulders.

Around two I left NaNa's and went back to Aaron's house.

"Hey A. What's up?"

"Nothing. I hardly ever see you anymore."

"Well, you know I be with my baby." I sit down on the chair. "He told me all yall and even Trill went out last night."

"Yeah."

"Yall could of called me."

"I thought you and Jeremy went out yesterday."

"Yeah we had a good time."

After I leave NaNa's, I go back to Aaron's and fix me something to eat. While I was finishing I get a call from Jeremy and he wanted to apologize for his actions the day before.

"I wanted to let you know I was sorry for what happened yesterday. I know it shouldn't have even gone down like that. I'm just feeling you in a way that you obviously ain't feeling me right now, but I understand you. I'm sorry."

"You cool. I'm sorry for overreacting like that though. It wasn't such a big deal."

"Alright. So, you think we can do something again before I go?"

"Yeah. What about going out to eat tomorrow or something?"

"Cool. I guess I'll talk to you tomorrow or you can call me tonight if you want to."

"Alright."

"Bye."

"Bye."

The next day Jeremy and I go out to eat and have fun. Then on Monday I get a call from Frank after I got off from work.

"Hey baby."

"I thought I told you not to tell anyone what I'm out here doing?"

"What you talking about?" I was truly confused.

"Ya boy Aaron came up to me talking noise. Talking about I better not get you caught up in my drug life and shit like that."

"It's not like Aaron going to disrespect you and tell everbody he knows."

"You already running your mouth too fucking much."

"What? All I did was tell NaNa, but I told her not to tell anybody else. All they doing is looking out for me."

"And I already told you that I didn't want anybody to know about it, and you told me you wasn't going to tell anybody."

I huff, "Look I understand where you coming from but..."

"But nothing. You lied and that's it. How can I trust you not to tell my shit anymore?"

"You can trust me Frank. I promise you I won't say anything else. I put my word on it that I won't tell anyone anything else. Please believe me baby."

"Listen I'll call you back later." He hangs up.

I look at my phone. "I know this dude did not just hang up on me." I then call up NaNa.

"Hello."

"I thought I told you not to tell Aaron about what I told you about Frank. I had already broken our trust when I told you, but then you go and tell Aaron."

"I know the life of a drug dealer's girl, and you ain't the type of person who wants to be living it. I know all the shit that goes in with it. You know everything I've been through and the only reason I told Aaron was because I was just looking out for you."

"Frank come calling me a little while ago saying how Aaron came up to him."

"Just know to keep it pushing no matter what happen."

"Yeah. I guess I'll talk to you later."

"Alright bye."

"Bye." I hang up the phone with her and continue on to Aaron's house.

When I get there is in the living room. I roll my eyes at him as I walk on my way to my room.

"What's wrong with you?"

I stopped and turn to face him. "Why you had to talk to Frank? He came at me telling me how you just walked up on him. Now he talking about because I told NaNa what he told me not to that he can't trust me. Yeah I know if I ain't want her to tell you, I shouldn't have told her in the first place, but it ain't your right to be going out and running your mouth to him. I know you my brother, but I'm a big girl now I can handle myself."

"You know I promised your ma and dad that I'll always look out for you. So I ain't going to stop now."

"But you need to cool down with that shit though. Just because you a little bit older than me don't mean you know better than me about the situation."

"When that nigga start fucking around on you, or something happen don't come crying to me about none of that shit." Aaron had got mad at what I said.

106

"I know ain't nothing going to happen, because Frank ain't like that."

He shakes his head and sits back in the chair.

I leave out of the living room and go to the room to pick out something to wear after I get out the shower. I put on some lounging shorts and a gray shirt that said sexy on the front, then I get out a black bra and some boy shorts. I pick up my deodorant and lotion off the dresser.

When I come from out of shower I saw that I had a missed call on my phone and it was no other than my baby, so I call him back.

"Yeah. What's up? Why you ain't pick up your phone?"

"I just got outta the shower." I sit down on the bed.

"You want to come over tonight?"

"Yeah I'll come over. Have you cooked something, because I haven't eaten since break today?"

"Yeah I cooked some spaghetti and meatballs with some garlic bread. Homemade."

"I most definitely will be over there in a minute. Do I need to bring some clothes or you going to kick me out tonight," I laugh.

"No you straight. I finished up business earlier today, and the other day I ain't kick you out. You said you were going to leave."

"Because I know you ain't want me there by myself."

"Well, yeah true."

"Shut up, you could have saved that for your thoughts," we both laugh. "I'll be over, after I get my clothes together for tomorrow."

"Alright. I'll see you when you get here."

"Alright baby bye."

"Bye."

I hang up and pack something to wear tomorrow to work and some other things. I get my things and cut off the light and leave out the room and go to the living room.

"I'm going over to Frank's house. I'll probably be back tomorrow afternoon or night. See you later."

"Bye." He does even look up from the TV.

I walk out the door and close it behind me, and go to the car. I put my bag in the backseat and crank up the car and drive off to Frank's house. When I get to the door, I ring the doorbell.

It was taking him a while to get to the door.

He finally opens the door. "Hey." He gives me a hug and takes my bag and we walked inside the house.

"What took you so long?"

"I was upstairs putting something up."

"Oh." We walk into the kitchen.

"You ready to eat?"

"Yeah, my stomach was growling on the way over here."

"Get a plate, because I ain't fixin' it."

"Ok. I'll do it myself." I walk past him to the cabinet. I take down a plate and fix some food. Then I go in the refrigerator and get some ice and tea. "When you going to teach me how to cook?" I walk over to the table and sit down.

"Friday." He sits down.

"Ain't you got to work?" I eat some of the spaghetti.

"I'm taking off that this week, because I'm going up to Brooklyn to see my pops Saturday morning and coming back Sunday night. You want to go?"

"I don't know."

"Come on. I want you to meet my dad."

"You're going up there on business or what?"

"No. I'm just going up there to see my dad."

"I was asking, because I'm not trying to be left in a hotel or wherever by myself." I take a drink of my tea.

"You know I wouldn't do you like that." He drinks some of my tea.

"You can fix your own."

He sits it down, "I made it."

"And." I eat some more of the spaghetti with the garlic bread.

"So I guess you like it, because you going hard on it."

"Shut up," I say playfully.

He looks into my eyes. "I never told you how pretty your eyes are."

"My eyes are like everybody else. Ain't nothing unique about them." I eat a piece of garlic bread.

"I like the shape of them. And they dark and pretty."

I finish up eating and we are sitting at the table talking.

"But seriously though. I'm sorry about what we talked about earlier. I should have kept my mouth shut.

I talked to Aaron about coming up to you like that. Sometimes he act like he somebody daddy or something, but I told him to cool out with that, so hopefully he will."

"You straight."

I get up and put my plate in the dish washer. "I'm about to go brush my teeth." I leave out the kitchen and Frank gets up. I go get my bag and take my tooth brush out and go to the downstairs bathroom to brush my teeth. I come back in the living room where Frank was sitting on the chair with one leg on the couch and one on the floor. I sit between them.

"Tomorrow I work the afternoon shift, so I go in at twelve." I take the remote from him and put it on the Starz channel and they were playing Love Jones. "This is my favorite movie. I have not seen this in a long time." The movie was already halfway through.

I take his arm from off the back of the chair and put it over my shoulder. He takes my other hand and plays with my fingers. And start kissing them.

I lean to the side and kiss him on the lips. "Now stop playing so I can watch the movie."

He keeps on at it, and now is kissing on my neck. "I got that same movie up stairs." He kisses my neck again. "We can watch that later." He takes the hand I was holding and rubs it up my body, and lifts my bra up and plays with my breast.

I sit up a little and unloosen my bra so he can get to them with ease. I then take my hands and wrap them around the back of his neck and bite my lip. "Mmm."

He starts pinching my nipples lightly and it sent a rush over my body. I moan, "Let's go upstairs, because afterwards I just want to lay up there."

"Alright." He lifts up a little pushing his rock hardness against my butt.

We walk up the stairs to the bedroom, I take my shoes off before getting on the bed. I get in the middle of the bed and take off my shirt and throw it on the floor.

"Strip baby." Frank cheers me on.

I stood up on the bed and started dancing for him. He turned on a Slow Jamz CD, and I started moving to R. Kelly's "Slow Whine". I dropped to my knees and roll my neck and move my body up and down.

In a sexy manner I remove my clothes, all the while dancing for him.

I took off my shorts last and threw them at Frank, then turned around and bent over in Franks face and he smacks my butt. He pulls my panties down with his mouth. After he gets them to my knees I take them off the rest of the way.

I go over to Frank and take off his shirt off while he undoes his belt buckle. He takes off the rest of his clothes, and then gets on the bed and lay down up under me.

"I want you to ride my face."

I slowly drop down, but then bring it back up just to tease him a little.

The song changes on the CD to Envouge's "Lose Control". This time I drop all the way down on his face. The feeling of his tongue felt so good, that I couldn't

111

help, but grind on his face when he put his tongue deep inside.

He wraps his arms around my thighs tightly, so that I wouldn't move when he started licking faster. I scream out. He made me cum so hard that I fell forward. That was the best one I ever had like that.

I move from his face down to his massive erection, and reach to his draw and pull out a condom out and open it and put it on him. Sliding down farther, he positions himself inside me. I start going up and down and working my hips on him trying not to go too fast. I never truly adjusted to his size, but the pain felt so good. I cried out in ecstasy.

I leaned forward and start nibbling on his ear to hold it in, but that didn't help.

I whispered to him in his ear, "I'm about to cum." My body started to shake as the pleasure came rushing out. When I catch my breath, I sit back up and turn around while he was still inside of me.

"Damn girl. You know just how to work this dick."

I lean all the way forward and stretched out, with my arm out in front of me and work him quite good, bouncing my juicy ass on his dick. He slaps my butt. After that he gets on top and does his thang with long deep strokes. He had me quivering and shaking under him. I wrap my legs around him and put my arms around his neck and hold on as he picked up his pace. He moved my hands from off of his neck and presses them down over my head.

He groans and keep on going at the same pace. I could tell he was reaching his point, so I start moving my hips with every motion and tighten up around him.

"Shit," he growl as he came so forcefully. He pulls out and lies next to me and throws the condom away in the trash can next to the bed.

I lay there trying to catch my breath. When I do I lean over on his chest and give him a kiss. I then get up and go to the bathroom and wash off and when I got back he had a towel over his body and was fast asleep.

Chapter 9

I wake up to Frank's hand playing between my legs. At first I thought I was dreaming.

"What are you doing?" I yarn.

"You were looking so sexy sleeping like that."

"I seriously thought I was dreaming. It felt like I came too."

"You did, I felt your pussy tightening up on my fingers like a few seconds before you woke up."

"Damn I sleep too hard. My shit is gone be swollen. I'm telling you I never had dick as big as yours."

"Quit lying." He was being modest.

"I'm for real. It be feeling so good." Both still naked, I straddle his body. "What you got planned for today?" I kiss him on the lips and sit back up.

"We can do whatever you want to?"

I bet putting him to sleep got something to do with doing whatever I want to do. "We can go shopping."

"We can do that. I want to buy you something if you going to New York with me. Are you going?"

"Yeah I want to go."

"You want to go out of town to the mall? I'll buy you whatever you want."

"Yeah, because I don't want to go to our mall. I'm tired of getting stuff from out of there."

"Ok." He pulls his self up with me still on top of him. "I'm about to go take a shower."

"I got to get my clothes from downstairs. I mine as well take a shower down there."

"You know you can take one with me."

"No. I'm good already. I know what you trying to do." I get off him and stand up and get ready to walk downstairs, and he slaps my booty.

I turn around. "Alright now." I go to his bathroom and get a towel and wrap it around me before I go downstairs.

After I take my shower and put on my clothes. I go upstairs and Frank was brushing his hair already dressed. I walk up behind him.

"You smell good baby."

"It's something new I picked up. You look good with your hair like that."

I had it all down with a part on the side. "Thank you."

"So you ready to go?" He turns to me.

"Yeah, so I can make it back time enough to go to work."

"We will."

"Are you ready?"

"Yeah I'm ready."

We leave out of the bathroom and he puts on one of his watches from off of the dresser, and gets his keys and we go down stairs. I pick up my purse and keys from the living room table and we head outside to the car after he locks up the house.

"Damn."

"What?" I ask.

"I left my other phone in the house. Here go the keys, I'll be right back." He takes the house key off the key chain and hands me the keys.

"Okay."

Frank goes back into the house and get his phone, and I get in the car. A few minutes later Frank comes out the house and get in the car. "You good?"

"Yes. You sho you got everything now?" I joke.

"Yeah. I got everything," he laughs.

"I'm ready to go."

He cranks up and we pull off and go on our way to the mall.

The trip was very interesting. Talking about what we liked about each other and some other things. When we get there I see these nice shoes and we go into the store.

"I need them." It was some cute sneakers that I really liked.

"Yeah they tough." He agrees with me.

"But they cost like 160 though." I look at the tag.

"So baby if you want 'em I'll get 'em for you. I told you I was going to pay for everything. Money's no object when it's for you." He grabs me around the waist and kisses me.

"Alright." I kiss him under his chin, because that's how much taller than me he was.

"Excuse me. Can I help yall?"

We turn around and he takes his arms from around me. "Yeah can I get these in a six.

"Yeah, I got you."

I hand him the shoes and he goes in the back and go look for them.

"You want something else from out of here."

"I ain't trying to spend up your money like that."

"I told you whatever you want, I got you."

"You sure, because I don't want it to seem like I'm with you for what you got."

"Whatever you want I got you. I ain't like these other dudes out here fronting and you know that." He kisses me on my forehead.

I start looking around for some more shoes in the boys section and Frank is looking around too. The sales person finally comes back with my shoes.

"Here you go."

I take the shoes from him. "Thank you."

"Ain't no problem ma."

"Can I get these too?"

"Yeah is there anything else you need, before I get these." He smiles.

"I'm sorry for running you back and forth, but these are the last ones."

Two or three minutes later he comes back with my shoes.

"Thank you."

"No problem."

I try them on and they fit perfectly.

"I'll have these up to the register when you are ready to checkout.

"Ok." I walk over to Frank, back in the men's section. "I found me another pair of shoes. You found some?"

"Yeah. I'm waiting for that girl to come back right now."

She comes back with the shoes.

"Her you go," she hands him them to him. "Do you want to try them on first."

"No, I'm good," Frank replies.

"Alright then, yall can come up front and check out."

We followed her up to the register, and he drops like five bills on us just at the shoe store. I haven't even spent that much money on myself in a shopping trip. Hey, he did say he was buying, so I'm spending.

Next we go to the clothing departments and I find a lot of good things. I found some nice clothes to match the sneakers that I got, but I also found some less casual clothes.

After we finish going to almost every store in the mall, and making a few trips back and forth, we leave and go back home. When we got back, I express my appreciation before I went in to work.

"Damn Miami. I never knew how good some men could be," I say to her.

"He got you glowing. Frank got that good, good huh?"

"Hell yeah. He took me shopping today and spent an ass load of money on me. We had a lovely time when we got home."

"No wonder you acting like that." Miami laughs.

"But how are you and Marc?" A customer comes up to my register.

"We straight now, since he started working. He was off today, so he kept Landon."

"At least he is working now. Thank you for shopping at Shoe Infinity. Please come back soon," I tell the customer after I ring her up.

"We've been getting a lot of business today, huh?"

"Yeah," as soon as I get the words out of my mouth. The boy I gave a fake number to came into the store.

"Oh my god," I whisper to Miami and nod my head towards the entrance.

He comes straight up to the counter over to me.
"What's up shawty?"

"Working." I say sarcastically.

"You ain't have to do me like that. All you had to do was say I couldn't get your number or whatever."

"Well, I'm sorry," I looked like I absolutely don't care. "So, are you going to buy something?"

"No, I just came in here to talk to you real quick."

"But what do we have to talk about?" I look him dead in the eyes.

"Can I take you out to eat one day?"

119

"Yeah, if my boyfriend can come too. Uhm, I ain't trying to be rude, but if you ain't buying nothing, you can get out of line and stop holding me up."

"Alright." He walked out of the store shamed.

"Dang girl. He don't get the point do he." Miami rings up some people.

"I know right. Shit, if I gave him the wrong number doesn't that mean something."

"How is everything with getting your place?"

"I'll be happy when they let me know something."

"They still ain't call you yet?"

I lean up against the counter. "No. He said it'll probably be a week or two before they'll call. I'm ready to be in my own place now. I might do what my aunt said and see about renting my mom's house out. I'm just trying to get from out of Aaron's house. It really doesn't seem like I am there that much now. I'm mostly at Frank's house."

"Ok. I'm about to leave soon as Rich come in."

"I am so mad at you." I huff.

"Why?"

"You leaving me here with that fool? I can't stand him. He swears he the shit, and that girlfriend of his is so clueless. He be cheating on her with everybody."

"She know it. She just don't want to leave that money he got," She stretches.

"Yep. He really has no reason to be working here."

"His mom and dad told him he had to get a job, or they were going to stop paying for college for him and stop depending on them for all his money."

"But they still give it to him anyways."

"Yeah."

Thirty minutes later Rich, who's real name is Richard, but Rich is what he is, comes in to work and Miami leaves and I'm there stuck with him.

"What's up sexy lady." He comes up to me.

"Hey Rich. What's good?" I say not even looking in his direction.

"Nutn much really. Trying to get you to be on my team."

"That would never happen. I ain't like none of them other girls you be talking to."

"You know you can't resist this." He steps back to show his self off. Wearing a fresh pair of sneaks and got his work outfit so iron till it's crispy and some big rocks in his ear.

"You are so fucking arrogant. Money can't getchu everything in life."

"It's keeping me a bad bitch on my side."

"If she was a real woman, she wouldn't be there just for the money."

"Man, fa get you Red. You ain't even that hot."

"I look better than the bitch you with. Don't trip, because you can't get with me."

He goes clock in and begin working, saying nothing else to me for the rest of the day.

When I leave work I go back over to Frank's house and stay until night and go back to Aaron's.

Chapter 10

Instead of leaving Saturday, Friday we take an early morning flight to Brooklyn, New York. This was my first time riding on a plane or even going this far from home, so I was kind of nervous. Being already scared of heights the turbulence wasn't a good feeling. I almost threw up, but I was ok.

When we finally landed at the airport, we got our luggage and his brother met us outside in his all black SUV.

He was also tall like Frank, and favored his mom. They greeted each other with some dap and a hug.

"What up little bru?" Frank says.

"We been keeping it pushing," he answers. "Who is this sexy lady?"

"My girlfriend Yolanda."

"Nice to meet you." I say

"And got that sexy southern accent."

"Thank you," I smile.

"My name is Brandon." He extends his hand for a handshake.

"Yall ready? It's going to be mad hectic if we don't get on the road now."

"Alright."

Frank puts our things in the back of his brother's truck, and we get out on the street.

New York looked like an exciting place, cars everywhere and huge buildings. Frank and his brother where talking up front while I was in the back enjoying the scenery.

When we got to where we were going. We pull up to a rather nice house, and an older guy came out onto the front porch. Right away I could tell it was their dad, because I could see the resemblance and could see where they got their good looks from.

When we stopped we all got out and the man came over.

"Hey dad, this is my girlfriend I been telling you about. Yolanda, this is my dad Peter."

"Hello." I say.

"Hey beautiful." He takes my hand and kisses it making me blush.

"Alright dad. You got to keep ya hands off." Frank interrupts jokingly.

His dad was quite the gentleman. We followed them inside of the house.

Frank whispers in my ear. "My dad likes younger girls, and I can tell he likes you."

"How can you tell?"

"I know the look. He tries to lure them in with his charm."

I make note as we walk inside, and into the living room.

"I see you have changed it up in here since the last time I visited."

"Yes thanks to that lovely finance of mine," Peter responds back to Frank.

"It's so beautiful in here," I say while admiring his lovely home.

"Thank you."

We sit down, and I sit right up under Frank, and he put his arm around my shoulder.

"Where your girl at B?"

"At her house. She wants me to come over now, but I told her I had to pick you up from the airport. So are yall staying here or getting a room?"

"Yall can stay here. It's more than enough of room." Peter insists. Frank looks to me for my answer.

"It's fine with me," I respond.

"I guess I'll go take our stuff out the back of your truck." Frank stands up. "I'll be right back baby."

"We'll help you. I need to talk to you anyway." Peter gets up and Brandon follows.

I sit inside waiting on them while they are outside talking. I pick up a picture off of the coffee table, and it was of Peter and a younger lady, she looked like she was in her mid-thirties. It looked kind of recent.

"Hello." I turned around and the woman I saw in the picture was walking down the stairs.

"Hello," I stand up.

"You must be Frank's girlfriend."

"Yes, I am Yolanda."

"I am Casey, Peter's fiancé," she extends her hand out to me.

I shake her hand. "Nice to meet you."

"The same here. So, yall are going to be here for the weekend?"

"Yeah, we are staying until Sunday night."

She nods her head. "I love your outfit, it's really cute."

"Thank you."

The men come back in the house from getting the bags and talking.

"So I see you met Casey," Frank stated.

"Yes I did."

He sits down next to me, and put his arm on the back of the chair, over my head.

Sam asks, "So how was your flight here?"

"Well, I didn't like it," I say.

"It was her first time flying." Frank says.

Casey says, "You'll get the hang of it. It's not so bad when you have flown more than once."

"Will you like something to drink or eat?" Sam asks.

"Something to drink please." I asked.

"Me too." Frank follows.

"Will you get us all a drink?"

Casey gets up and goes over to the bar and starts making us some drinks.

Frank turns to me. "I want to take you around today and show you a couple of places."

"Ok. I'm down."

She comes back with the drinks and we sit and talk for a while until Frank is ready to leave and go out in the city.

He takes me all over New York, also taking me to the house he used to live in when he was growing up, in Queens. It was in a very bad neighborhood with police roaming up and down the block, and at the store corners.

He pulls over next to the house.

"I remember the days." I could see him reflecting on his past. "We went through a lot in that house. Been robbed, eviction notices, lights turned off, bad living. That's what started my dad to hustling. He was trying to make a better life for his family.

When he first started getting money, we moved into a better house in Brooklyn. We were doing good, the money coming in like crazy." He smiles and chuckles.

"My dad's status got so high that he went into business of his own, because he was the best running these streets. With that came the flashy cars, clothes, and the cheating on my mom. Word got out quick about him in the game. I was in a private school in elementary, and because I was Peter Johnson's son the other kid's parents wouldn't let them play with me.

When my mom's found out about him cheating, she packed me and my brothers up and we moved down south where my mom was from. She had got a job and we had to start over with what money he gave her. He used to fly me and my brothers up here every summer and every break we had. I loved being up here with him. When I was fifteen I started getting in trouble. In and out of juvenile for stealing, fighting, and other stuff, so she sent me back up her so he could deal with me.

And when I was sixteen, I dropped out of school, so my dad put me in the business. My other brothers stayed with mom until they finished school and moved up here, and that's when they both got in."

I grab his hand.

"My youngest brother had got this girl pregnant and she had my nephew and niece. He was happy, but still in love with the game. On his 22nd birthday, he went out in the wrong neighborhood by his self and someone shot him three times, twice in the chest and once in the head. That night after we found out, she dropped the kids off at my dad's old girl house so she could watch them. The next day we found her dead, because she had overdosed on some of his heroin and pills. She had a note beside her that said, *I left to be with Tyrell.*

After they buried the two of them my mom took full custody of the kids. That shit broke me down for a minute. That pushed me to sell and be the best like my dad. When I got enough status I moved back and bought my mom her house, and mine. I got my cousins Boobie and Stretch, and my close friend I was the lead man staying low key, while they remained on the forefront."

He clears his throat. "I ain't even going to lie to you, I ran through a few girls, but all they were in for was the money, so I had to let them go. Working at Club X was the backup thing to stay low key but I know I needed something else to justify the money I had coming, so I started up a car wash out on the west. You know Speedy Wash?" Frank asks me.

"Yeah, I go there sometimes, but I never knew you owned it. You must never be there?"

"Nah, I got an old school cat running the spot for me. Him and my pops was tight back in the day, so I trust him to run my business right. I stop through time from time to collect my money. I generate a lot of business there. You can get your car washed and detailed, and get a little something extra if you know what I mean."

"Yeah I feel ya."

"The first time I saw you at the club, you caught my eye." He smiles. "You was dating ole boy then though, and yall was too young to be in the club. I even met your dad before he died. I went to his funeral to show my respect. I was cool with him."

"I didn't know you were there. Probably because I was crying so much," I chuckle.

"Yeah. I sat in the back row. That's when you slacked up on coming out to the club. I missed talking to you and seeing your pretty face."

I smile.

"I was so happy when you finally gave me a chance. I truly love you Yolanda and I want you to always know that."

"I love you too baby. You know the only issue I had with you was that for one I was with Ace and the age difference. But I got over that, because why was I being crazy to almost let a fine ass man like you go."

Frank turns to me and gives me a kiss on the lips. "You ready to go back to my Dad's?"

I nodded my head.

When we get back to the house, Peter and Casey were in the living room laughing while watching something on TV.

Frank and I went straight up stairs and washed up.

"How'd you liked today?" He asks when we got into bed.

"It was nice. I liked how you let me in and let me understand where you were coming from. I'm glad you trust me enough to let me know about everything."

"I feel that I can trust you, besides that little fuck up when you spoke on the shit I do, and Aaron came to check me about it."

"I'm sorry for that, for real. I talked to NaNa about it, because she knows the life of being with a dude like you. Even though Damien and on the same level you are."

"I'll take it as a mistake, but don't make another." He kissed my hand. "So tell me some more about you. I want to who is Yolanda not Applez. I want to know your dreams, where you see yourself in the next few years."

"Well Yolanda is you regular female. I sometimes can be insecure about things, and feel like I need validation from others. I'm sometimes shy and second guess myself at times. As far as dreams, I want to go to school and become a registered nurse, but I also want to take classes to become a social worker to help at risk people, drug addicts, and kids. It's a lot that I want to do."

"Well, why you ain't doing nothing about it?"

"I mean, I did plan to go to college like the beginning of the next year after I had graduated from high school, but after things got really bad with me and my mama, I put things off."

"You don't have nothing but time now. You can't sit and think you can depend on no one else to get you to where you want to be. You got to work hard for want. You got to go in it with a hustles mentality and get it at any means if it means that much to you."

I nod my head while taking in everything that he was telling me.

"I'm really glad you came with me for real."

"Me too."

"Can I ask you something?"

"Have you ever or will ever have a threesome?"

"No and no. I can't share my man with another chick. I'll get jealous because you'll be giving that good dick up right in my face, and I don't want another female feeling on me or nothing."

"It'll be fun and different."

"Have you done did it before?"

"Once. It was real cool."

"Mieko told me about a threesome he had with these two chicks, and the type of shit they were doing just ain't for me. Plus I ain't trying to lose you to nobody else."

"Why would I ever want to let you go baby?" He kisses me sticking his warm tongue in my mouth. He started rubbing on my body making me want him so bad

       "No Frank. What about your dad and Casey? You know I can get loud."

       "So, I want you. Who cares if they hear? They shouldn't be listening anyway." He kisses my neck.

       I laugh. "You are so crazy baby." I was ready too, and Frank knew it. He took off my shirt and bra.

       "So you just going to take it?" I say naughtily.

       "It's mine right?" He raised his eyebrow.

       Continuing his antics, he unbuttons his pants and takes them off and sits back down. I pull up his shirt, and take it off and start rubbing and licking all over his chest and abs. Frank reaches over to turns on the stereo to drown out some sound of our love making.

Chapter 11

"Wake up baby," he kisses me.

"Good morning," I stretch, "How long you've been up." I look at the clock and it was 11:13 a.m.

"Since 7:00. I've been out for a little bit"

"Oh." I sit up.

"I went and visited a few old friends."

"Business." I pull my hair back.

"Some. You want me to cook you some breakfast while you get ready?

"Could you please?" I get up out the bed so I get a towel and my clothes and went out to the bathroom in the hall. And Frank goes to the kitchen.

I take quick shower and get dressed and do my hair, then go down stairs to something that smelled so good.

"It smells good in here," I sit down at the table.

"French toast, bacon, and juice." He sits my plate in front of me, and he sits down with his.

"I hope we get to do something today, I really would like to see the city up close without viewing it from the car." I begin eating.

"We are."

"Where is your dad and Cassie?" I drink some of my juice.

He puts his fork down. "Out. Brandon and his wife are coming by. She's seven months pregnant and bitchy. Well, she was like that before she got pregnant."

"How old is he anyway?" I start back eating.

"He's twenty-six and she is twenty-four.

"What is she having?"

"A girl."

"Is he ready to become a dad?"

"Yeah. He wanted a boy though."

"Am I asking you too many questions?"

He laughs. "No."

"You can be honest and say if I am."

"Well yeah."

I pop him on his arm. "Shut up. I ask because I like to know things instead of just assuming."

"But that's still nosy."

"Nah."

The doorbell rings.

"I'll be right back." He gets up from the table.

"Ok."

I finish what all I was going to eat and take it to the garbage disposal. I put my plate and cup in the dishwasher.

When Frank comes back his brother and his wife is behind him.

"Hello," I greet them.

"Hey Yolanda," Brandon responds, "this is my wife Carmen."

"Yeah," she says with attitude. She sits down holding her side, and Brandon is trying to help her. "I got this," she snaps.

"Well damn."

"Ugh." She rolls her eyes.

Frank whispers to me, "Don't mind her."

"She do not know."

"So you like it up here so far?" Brandon says as he sits down by his wife.

"Yes it's been ok."

"Would you ever move up here?"

"I like that good Georgia dirt. I mean it's a good place to come visit, but not for me to stay." I smile.

My phone rings and it's NaNa.

"I'll be right back baby."

"Okay."

I go to our room.

"Hey NaNa."

"What's up girl?"

"You know. Just chillin.

"What's it like up there?"

"We are staying at his dad's house. I swear this house is a freakin mansion. Five bedroom and four baths. It is so pretty."

"Is his dad cool?"

I sit down on the bed. "Yeah and he is very nice looking to be an older guy. His dad's fiancé is like thirty something. I met his brother and he is a looker too.

"No now."

"Yes. He picked us up from the airport yesterday. Him and his wife here right now. She's seven months pregnant and a bitch".

"Oh."

"So what's going on down there?"

"Same thing from when you left. I was calling because you ain't call me like you said you would."

"Frank took me around yesterday. He took me to the house he grew up in. After we got back home we talked some more, then it went down."

"In his dad's house?"

"Yeah. We had to turn on the stereo and turn it up, because we was so loud in here."

"Damn. So, what yall got planned for today?"

"I'm not sure I just know I want to do something."

"Get me something, please. I'll pay you back when you get back."

"Alright I'll call you back later."

"Ok girl. Have fun."

"I will. Bye."

"Bye."

After I get off of the phone, I join everyone in the living room.

Talking to Frank I say, "That was NaNa."

"What kind of name is NaNa?" Carmen rudely says.

"It's a nickname." I sit down.

"More like gehttofide."

"Shut up. You need to stop acting like that." Brandon gets back at here.

"For real. Because…no…let me calm down and keep my peace."

Frank says, "I told you not to worry about her."

"Yeah, yeah." I roll my eyes.

"What yall doing today." Franks says to Brandon.

"Same old shit. Chillin at the house and on that work."

"I feel ya on that man. I hope them fucks ain't messing up back home."

"Ain't Boob and Stretch putting in work?"

"Stretch been half assing lately. I'm going to have to let Black and him switch positions until he can come back up on his game."

This was the first time I'd ever heard Frank talk like this in front of me.

"If I had my mans up here, I could get some work back down."

"I can get you one of my workers for the job. He's real reliable. You want me to call him up and let him know?"

Frank looks at me, then back at Brandon.

"I got to get back to you on that one."

He promised me this wasn't a business trip, but I could tell it was turning into just that.

"Baby, what time are we going out?" I ask.

"Don't worry, we going soon. Oh yeah, I want to take you to this hot club in Harlem. I'm going to see if you can hang with them."

136

"You already know I can."

"Sounds childish." Carmen buts in.

"How old are you?"

"Twenty-four," she says with confidence.

"You've been to college."

"No but I plan on to."

"So you pregnant, 24, haven't been to college, bitchin, and you nagging and complaining, but you sitting here calling me childish."

"Well, where your diploma at?"

"Believe me boo, I'm going to that very soon. I done respected you from all your little smart comments, but believe me boo, you ain't got nothing over me. Frank, can we go, because I swear…"

"Alright come on." He stands up.

I get walk with my head held high pass Carmen.

We go out to the garage and get his dad's new BMW that he left us the keys to. It was black with the stock rims still on it. It was a very nice car. It was four other cars in there too, all of much value.

"Your dad got a good taste in cars." I say opening the door to get in.

"Yeah. He still thinks he's young, buying all this stuff."

"I would too if I had it like that."

We pull out of the garage and head down the driveway on our way to the stores. We walk around and he buys me some things. After we get finished shopping we got to eat at this restaurant. After we come back home we chill around before we get ready to hit up the club out in Harlem.

"How do I look?" I turn around for him.

I have on an outfit that I brought from the mall when we went the other day.

"You look good like always baby."

"Well, I like what you got on too. Do they play any music from down south up here?"

"Yeah, but mostly music from here."

"Ok." I finish with my makeup and spray some perfume on.

"You ready?"

"Yeah baby." I slide into my heels.

We leave out of the house and take the same car from earlier to the club. When we got there it was all types of people in there. A girl walks up to us soon as we get in.

"Hey what's up Frank? You back in town I see."

"Yeah, I just brought my girl up here to show her a good time. Apples this is Ta'nesha, Ta'nesha Applez."

"Hello." I say.

"Hey, but it was nice seeing you Frank."

"Alright."

She walks away.

"Baby will you get me a drink? You know I can't go get my own yet."

"You know I got you."

We go over to the bar and Frank orders two drinks. A Strawberry Dakari for me, and a Heineken for him.

"Baby, you going to dance tonight?"

"Yeah. I'm going to show you how we do it up here."

138

When we finished our drinks me and him hit the dance floor. He went back and chilled at the bar while I danced some more.

"Baby girl you got mad flavor. Where you from?"

"Georgia."

"What you doing all the way up here?"

"My boyfriend brought me."

Frank walks over.

He jumps. "Oh Frank, this your girl?"

"Yeah."

"My bad."

He walks away.

"You know him?" I ask.

"No, but everybody still knows me. They know not to fuck with it."

He puts hands on my butt and kisses me. We stayed at the club a while longer then headed back home. We washed up and got into bed.

"Did you have a good time?" He runs his hand through my hair.

"Yeah I did."

"You always find a way to get attention."

"I'm just a people's person." I laid my head on his chest.

"I see that."

I put my left leg over him.

He kissed me on the forehead. "You know you can get all the way on if you want to."

"I'm cool."

"But I like it when you sleep on top of me."

"I do too."

He puts his hand on my waist and pulls me on top of him.

I sit up and could feel his hardness growing under me. "I see what you want." I rub my hand down the bridge of his nose.

He sits up on the bed and pulls my night shirt from under me and tells me to lean back. He pulls my thong to the side and starts playing with my pussy.

"Nice and wet," He says.

I smile. "Mhm."

He puts two fingers inside of me, while he uses his thumb to play with my clit.

I moan then bite my lips.

He starts hitting my spot and it sent my body up the wall. He keeps going until he makes me cum.

"Damn girl." He replies.

I lay that way until I could catch my breath.

I sit back up and pull down his boxer shorts. I kiss him from his lips all the way down his chest until my chin brushed against his dick. I had never gave anyone oral sex, but from the look of things, he seemed to be enjoying it. He was moaning and grunting and he kept his hand holding the back of my head, and would keep moving my hair from out of his sight.

"Damn girl, you about to make me cum. Shhhit!"

Before he could erupt in my mouth, I jacked him off to his point.

We clean up and before I could get to bed he was nodding. I get into bed and give him a kiss on the cheek, and lay my head on his chest and drifted off to sleep.

The next day, we were getting ready to go. I really enjoyed our time together out of town.

"Thank you for your hospitality," I give Peter a hug.

"You're welcome. I hope Frank brings you back one day."

"I hope so too. I like it up here."

"Alright, we need to get going before our flight leaves." Frank rushes.

"Ok. I'm not going to hold yall up any longer."

"See you later dad."

"Bye Mr. Peter."

"You can call me dad."

"Well bye...dad."

We go inside the airport and they were just starting to board people on our plane, so we run to the boarding area after we give them our luggage.

Back in Georgia.

He had his cousin Boob to leave his Range Rover at the airport. So, we go to his house for a while then he takes me to my house.

When I get inside I plug my phone to the charger, because my battery was dead. I turned it on and I had a text from Jeremy.

Jeremy-

Wats up Applez? Wat you doing?

Me-

Just got back 4rm NY with Frank.

Jeremy-

Wat yall was up dey 4?

141

Me-

Nosy.. we just went 2 visit his dad.

Jeremy-

Wat all yall did?

Me-

He took me round & out to da club.

Jeremy-

You had fun?

Me-

I did. 2 much fun.

Jeremy-

2 much fun doin ole buddy huh?

Me-

Shut up I had fun n general :P

Jeremy-

Ok.

Me-

What you up 2???

Jeremy-

Out wit my homies, thinking about you.

Me-

O 4 real???

Jeremy-

Yeah

Me-

When u coming back down here?

Jeremy-

I dnt kno

Me-

How u & ur gurl doin?

Jeremy-

The same. We stay arguing

Me-

About wat?

Jeremy-

Dumb shit.

Me-

I'll call or text you later, bc I got to let bruh know I'm back.

Jeremy-
Oh alright

I stop texting him and call Aaron off of my house phone, to let him know I was back and ok. Then I call NaNa and she say she is coming over.

When she comes over we sit in the living room and talk about my trip.

NaNa sits down. "What's up girl?"

"Nothing much, just tired though." I sit down beside her.

"You had a good time?"

"Yeah, but his brother wife was getting on my last nerve with all her complaining and shit. They got her too spoiled. She tried going off on me, but I let her know quickly I ain't the one.

"I know this girl from up there that act just like that too."

"You want something to drink? Some water, soda or something?"

"I'm cool."

I pick up the remote and turn on the TV, and The Color Purple was on.

"They play this movie everyday seem like," I say sitting the remote on the sofa. "So what yall got planned for my Birthday Friday?"

"I don't know. I was thinking about having you a party at the club or something."

"I just want to have a good time since it's going to be my twenty first and all. And oh yeah, I did get your outfit" I stand up. "I'll be right back."

143

I go to the room and get the bag that NaNa's clothes are in, and come back out.

"Here you go." I hand it to her.

She takes it out of the bag. "This is so cute. I ain't really think you was going to get nothing."

"You can find your own shoes, but you can find the receipt in the bottom so you can know exactly how much to pay me back."

"Ok. I got you." She laughs.

"I got an outfit that I can ware on my birthday too. About to be looking extra sexy. I'm going to go get my hair and nails done."

"Frank paying for it?"

"If he want to. I don't even think I told him when it is. Let me call him right now."

I pick up my cell phone and dial Frank's number.

"Hello?"

"What's up baby?"

"Just got out the shower. What you up too?"

"NaNa is over here and we was just talking about my birthday that is this Friday. She was talking about maybe having a party Saturday. I was wondering would you pay to get my hair and nails done?" I ask.

"Yeah baby. You know I got you."

"Thank you. Do you got to work that night?"

"I'm going to take that night off, because I want to party with you."

"You better, but anyways I guess I'll talk to you later."

"I I'll be over there tomorrow morning."

"I guess I'll see you then."

"Alright."

144

"Alright bye." I end the call and put my phone down.

"So he said yeah?" NaNa asked curiously.

"Yes, well that part's finished."

"I'm going to have everything planned. I'm going to call about the club tomorrow to make sure."

"Ok."

"Yeah, well, I'm about to get back home so I can go back to Damien. We got to something poppin off for tonight." NaNa stands up. "So I'll get at you later."

"Ok girl. I'll walk you to the door." I get up, and we walk to the door, and she leaves.

Around nine 'o clock I get a call from Jeremy. We talk for about an hour or two. He said his girlfriend was at her mom's house. I invited him to my birthday party on Saturday, and he said he would be there. So I guess NaNa will have everything set for my big day, and all I have to do is be there.

Chapter 12

Today was my birthday and I was so excited about celebrating with everyone, but I hadn't been able to get in touch with Frank all day. I left a message on his answering machine. "What's up baby? I've called a few times. I hope you don't disappoint by not showing up. Love you much and give me a call back." I end the call and let out a deep sigh.

"He's still not answering?" NaNa asks.

"No. He's probably coming though. At least he told me he would."

"Don't worry about him. It's your birthday, and we about to have some fun." She bumps me.

"Yeah."

"You need to hurry and get ready. You don't want to be late to your own party."

I put on my heels and we go into the living room.

"Dang Applez, you looking fine as fuck girl." Mieko states.

"Thank you." I say with a fake smile.

I fix myself up in the mirror.

"You are looking good." Aaron says

"Thank you."

"Yall ready now?" Aaron asks.

I shake my head. "Yeah."

We all head out the door and I lock the door behind us.

I tell Aaron, "Yall going to follow us."

"Alright."

The girls get in my car and the dudes rode with Aaron. When we get to the club, I find a parking space, and we walk off in the club. I enter first.

The DJ says, "Ok. Here she is birthday girl. What up Red?"

I throw my hands up. "What up Twist?"

"Come here baby girl"

I go over to the DJ booth.

"Yall know what it is. You want to say something?"

I grab the mic. "What's up everybody. I wanna thank yall for coming out for my party. Now it's time to fucking turn up!" I leave the DJ booth and go over to the bar to get a drink to start my night off.

The bartender hands me my drink.

"Thank you."

Miami says, "I'm about to go dance. Are you going to be alright?"

"Yeah, I'm cool. I'm just going to sit here for a minute, until I finish my drink."

When she leaves Jeremy comes over.

"Why you looking so sad? Ain't you supposed to be having fun?

"Yeah." I give him a hug. "I'm just mad at Frank because he was supposed to be here, and I haven't talked to him since Thursday morning."

"You ain't got to be sad, because I'm here now." He sits down beside me.

I start smile. "You always find a way to make me smile.

"That's what I'm here for."

I drink some of my drink.

"You looking sexy for real though."

"Thank you. You looking pretty good yourself."

"You want to go dance?"

I drink the last of my drink. "Yeah." I get up and begin walking to the dance floor, and I can tell Jeremy was looking at my booty.

I turn around. "Damn can I get my ass back?"

He laughs.

We go out and dance.

"I swear Yolanda you looking good as fuck. I ain't even gonna lie you got me horny."

"Well, I can't help you with that."

He pulls me closer to him. "You feel that?"

"Hell yeah. I got to quit fucking with you, because you going to get me in trouble. On some real shit.

"I'm going to quit."

"I need another drink."

"I got you."

We go back over to the bar and Jeremy buys me a drink.

"Fuck man." Jeremy smiles.

"What?"

"Man, you looking sexy as fuck, for real."

I take a sip of my drink. "You are too much."

"Can I ask you something?"

"Yeah." I turn my chair to him.

"If you wasn't with ole buddy, would I be somebody you would want?"

"Oh my god Jey. I thought we done been through this before. You already know the situation"

"Yeah."

"So. Anyways, Trey and his ole lady could of came."

"They don't really go out like that since they had they kids." He drinks some more of his drink.

"Ok. Let them know they could of came though."

I spot one of my male friends coming over.

"What's up Marc?" I set my drink down.

"You ma. Can I get a dance?"

"I'll be right back Jey."

"Yeah. I'm about to get back out there too."

"Ok."

"Come on." Marc says as he grabs my hand.

Marc brings me out on the dance floor. They are playing Jim Jones "Certified Gangsta" and I was doing my thing. I started dancing with a lot more people, and with NaNa and Miami. I also did a sandwich with Aaron and Mieko.

"I'll be right back." I tell Miami.

"Ok."

I go to the bathroom and call Frank's phone.

"Yeah, so business is better then your girl? Call me when you can." I close the phone and go to the bar and get a shot.

NaNa and Miami comes over.

NaNa says, "Where you went?"

"To the bathroom. He told me he was coming and now he want even pick up his phone."

"Don't worry about him and just have some fun."

"You looking too pretty to be looking so sad," says Miami.

"I know right. I must be trippin."

I get back out on the dance floor.

I have my last dance with Jeremy. We didn't leave the club until closing time, and I was oh so tipsy. So much that Miami had to drive us back to my house. Jeremy came over too. Aaron drove Miami back home.

"I am so fucked up right now, and I'm hungry as hell." I sit down on the arm of the chair.

"I'm hungry too." Jeremy says.

"I'm about to warm up some takeout I got earlier. You can have some."

"Ok."

He sits down and I go to the kitchen and heat up the food, I grab two forks and come back into the living room.

We eat and talk a while, then I start getting sleepy.

I yard. "I'm about to go brush my teeth and go to bed.

"I'll just crash right here."

"You can get in bed too, but sleep on top of the covers and I'll give you a blanket."

"Yeah. That's straight."

"Come on." I walk toward the room, and he follows behind me.

I go to the bathroom and brush my teeth and switch into some pajama shirts and tank top.

"Ok. You need to get your ass right in this bed." I say kind of slurred.

"Can I take my shirt off? I mean I got tank top under this."

"Yeah go ahead."

I go over to my closet and take down a blanket.

"Here you go." I throw the blanket at him.

He laughs.

"Don't be getting fresh either."

"I'm not. I'm going to be a good boy."

"Yeah whatever."

I get in the bed and turn on the stereo. I lay on my stomach and turn my head away from Jeremy and go to sleep.

At 7:00 am I wake up with my face very close to Jeremy's, nearly touching. I studied his face. His skin was so smooth and even, and he had cute nose and sexy lips.

Jeremy begins to open his eyes. He jumps and quickly moves away.

"Good morning." He says.

"Morning."

151

"How long you been up?"

"A few seconds. I was just noticing how you got all the way on my side."

"Oh, sorry. I'm use to sleeping on that side."

"You straight though."

"I guess I should be getting back."

"Ok."

He sits up and moves the cover from off of him. I notice his tattoo on his back as he bent over and put on his shoes.

"Can I see your tattoo?"

"Yeah." He pulls his shirt up.

It is a lion for his astrology sign Leo.

I trace my hand across his back. "I like that."

"Thank you." He pulls his shirt down and put on his other shirt.

"I would get up and walk you to the door, but my head is hurting."

"I'll call you later today."

"Alright."

He stands up.

"Lock my door behind you." I yell to him as he leaves out my room door.

"I got you."

"Bye."

"Bye."

He leaves and I go back to sleep.

Three and a half hours later I get woke up by some knocks at the front door. I get up and go see who it is.

'Who in the hell is this at the door?' When I open it I put my hands over my eyes to block the sun because my head was hurting. I look up and it's Frank.

Chapter 13

I opened the door all the way so that he could come in. I go sit on the couch and he follows.

"What's up?" Frank says as he sits down.

"What was up with you last night?"

"Come on baby, don't trip off that."

"What you mean don't trip? You told me you was going to be there. I had been calling you for two days and you ain't been answering your phone, and now you want to show up like ain't nothing wrong. I guess I ain't as important to you as some other things." I roll my eyes at him.

"I'm sorry. I was busy."

"Yeah, whatever."

"Please don't start this shit. I'm here now ain't I?"

"But today ain't yesterday."

"Don't start with me!"

"What?" I sit up in the chair.

"You heard me."

"I don't know how you are used to females you used to dealing with, but I ain't gonna take to much of you hollering at me. You can take some of that bass up out your voice."

He puts his hands around my throat

"Frank." I grab at his wrist.

"What you was saying now? Huh? I guess you ain't so big now. If I wasn't there ain't no second guessing me." He tightens up.

"Stop," I say gasping for air.

"You need to learn how to keep your fucking mouth close sometimes. So don't talk to me like that again." He pushes me to the floor, and I scramble over to the couch.

Tears were flooding from my eyes.

"Get up." Frank ordered.

I stand.

"I'm sorry." He hugs me and I cry on his shoulder. "I've been having a lot of stress on me and your nagging ain't helping. Work coming up short from Stretch and all."

We sit down on the couch.

Sniffling. "I just expected you to be there for me last night." I wipe away my tears.

"I'm sorry I wasn't there. How was it?"

"It was nice. Except there were some people about to fight. Besides that it was fun. I took pictures."

"Go get 'em so I can see them.

"Ok." I get up and go to the room to get the pictures I took at the party and come back and show him.

"Damn baby, you was looking sexy as hell."

I wipe my eyes and nose with the back of my hand.

He keeps flipping through the pictures.

"I did wear it for you."

"I like this one right here."

It was a picture of me turned around showing off my booty.

"You can get it."

Frank phone goes off with a text message. "I'll be right back." He got up and walked outside.

It was raining outside so I decided to clean up the house. While I was leaning up in the living room, I find Frank's phone on the chair after he spent the previous day at my house. On his phone is a text from earlier that day. It said from Melisa, so I open it to see what was up.

From: Melisa
What's up baby? Are you coming
through tonight?? I want you 2 put your
face n it like u did the other day. Ha!
Ha! Get @ me later boo....
10:11 a.m.

I get so heated that I check all of his messages. It was a lot of sexual comments on there from the same girl and another one. After I read all of them, I checked his sent messages.

Frank had two phones, so obviously he ain't realize he left this one at my house.

"Oh, I'm about to pay him a visit." I grab up my keys and both of our phones and lock the door behind me as I leave out the door.

When I get there I see another car in his driveway. I go up to his door and unlock it with a key he had given me.

It was silent down stairs except from the sounds that were coming from upstairs. It was the sounds of a woman moaning and screaming. I walk up the stairs with a normal speed and open his door to his room, and stand there for a few seconds.

I was shocked by what I saw. He was hitting some girl from the back, so they didn't notice me there.

I clear my throat and he turns around surprised.

"Here go your fucking phone." I throw it at his head, but he ducks and it hits the wall.

I run back down stairs, then I think again, and I go back up stairs and go after the girl while she was trying to put on her clothes. I jump across the bed and start boxing her all in the face, and she tries to fight back, but I had her.

Frank tries to pull me off of her, but I had her by her, hair pulling out some of her tracks. She gets loose when Frank has me up in the air holding me.

I shake loose trying to catch my breath. "How could you do this shit to me? And yeah I read all your

messages. You was with that bitch on my birthday too."
I started fighting him. Punching him and hitting him in
the face one good time.

He finally slaps me after he had gotten enough.
I hit the floor from the force of his hit.

"Don't ever hit me like that again. I don't know
who told you to look in my phone in the first place."

I get up. "You got me looking stupid for you,
while you running around fucking all these other
bitches." I take a deep breath. "I feel so stupid because
of you."

"You should feel stupid."

"Fuck you. You bitch."

He punches me in the lip and I hit his bed
motionless, and he leaves out of the room.

Blood was coming from my lip and I could feel
my lips instantly swelling. I get up holding my mouth. I
run downstairs crying, and leave out the front door
while he was sitting in the living room watching TV like
shit ain't just went down. I go get in my car and call up
NaNa.

"Hey girl what's up."

"You was right." I sniffle.

"Was right about what? Girl, what's going on?"

"I caught him cheating. I'm going to come over
to your house in a minute alright."

"Okay."

I hang up with her and head on to her house.
When I get to her house I knock on the door, and a
moment later she comes to the door.

"What happened girl?" She lets me inside.

158

"When me and ole girl was fighting I hit my lip on something when I jumped across his bed." Lying.

"How it all started."

We sit down on her couch.

I wipe my nose. "See he left his other phone at my house the night before and I looked at it and he had a message from someone named Melisa. So I got mad and read it. She was saying how she wants him to come through and wanted him to put his face in it like he did the other night. So I'm like what the fuck? That's when I read all of his messages, and he had two other chicks in there besides that one, saying all types of sexual stuff. And them days I couldn't get hope to him, he was out fucking, and on my birthday at that. So I was going over there to give him his phone, and when I got there I used the key he gave me and went inside. I head the noises from down stairs so I went up there and opened the door. They didn't hear me because he was fucking her from behind, so I cleared my throat."

I take a deep breath trying to fight back the tears. "I threw his phone at his head, but he ducked and it hit the wall. I ran back down stairs and though for a second and went backed up there and jumped on her, and he grabbed me up off of her. She ran off an we was fussing or whatever and I started hitting him, and he pushed me off of him and told me to get out."

"I told you you wasn't cut out to be in the position to be a dope boys girl. Believe me Damien done did me dirty plenty of times, but I realized them other bitches wasn't nothing, because they was giving it up easy. See I brought more to the table and he eventually quit doing it when he saw what he had at home."

"But it still shouldn't be like that. The messed up thing about it is that I still love him, and I don't know if I want to leave him or stay.

"If you really do, you better choose quick and do whatever you can to get and keep him."

I sit back in the chair.

"You want me to get some ice?"

"Yeah."

NaNa gets up and go get me some ice and comes back.

"Thank you. I'm about to go. I'll see you later"

"Alright." She stands up.

We walk over to the door and I leave.

When I get back home, I sit for and think about what NaNa said and then I call up Frank.

"Yeah." Frank answers the phone.

"I'm sorry for going through your phone and hitting you, and everything." Not really knowing what should I be sorry for. "I should of called before coming over too. I'm real sorry baby."

"You think a few sorrys going to make me forgive you."

"I am though. I love you and I'm willing to do anything to make it up to you I told you I was down for you."

"Look, I'll come through after while and we can talk then."

"Ok baby. I love you."

He hung up before saying anything else. When Frank came over, he apologized for his actions and for whatever reasons I forgave him. I had indeed fallen in love with Frank, but if this was what I was going to have

160

to put up with, I didn't know how long our relationship would last.

Frank promised to me that he wouldn't cheat on me and he would do better with setting aside time for me when it came to him and being in the streets.

My phone ringed and since he was closer to it, he checks the caller ID. "Aaron." Then gives me the phone

"What's up Applez."

"Nothing much."

"We was going to the movies, you want to go?"

"Yeah. I'll be over in a minute then."

"But it don't start till…"

"I know." She laughs trying to hide the conversation. "I'll be there."

"Alright." He could tell I was acting strange. "Why you acting like that?"

"I'll let you know."

"You need me to come over or something."

"No, I'm good."

"I'll see you later."

"Alright bye." I end the conversation and pass it to Frank to put back on the charger.

"So, you about to leave in a minute?"

"Yeah after I get dressed."

He nods his head. "Well I'm about to go. I'll talk to you later."

I sit up and he stands up and I follow him to the door.

He kisses me on the forehead, and walks off without even saying bye. I close the door behind him and sit on the couch and call back Aaron.

Aaron answers, "Yeah."

"I ain't going to be able to make it. The reason why I said yeah and was acting like that is because I was trying to get rid of Frank. He gets on my nerves sometimes."

"I just got off the phone with NaNa." Go figure. "She told me what happened."

"Please don't say I told you so, because I don't want to hear it. I already know."

"I told you I was going to chill, but you okay though?"

"Yeah, I couldn't be any better," saying sarcastically.

"You know if you need me I'm right here."

"Yeah, I know."

"Alright, I'll talk to you later."

"Bye."

After I get off of the phone with Aaron, I go to my room to take a nap. Thirty minutes later my phone rings and it was playing the ringtone I set for Jeremy.

Rolling onto my back I answer, "Hello."

"What you doing?"

"I was sleeping."

"You want me to call you back later then?"

"No, you good."

"Ok."

"You had a good day?"

"Until I got home from school. She was talking noise before she left for work."

I sit up. "Oh."

"What about you?"

"It was terrible."

"Why? What happened?"

"Well, first off this morning…" I explain everything, leaving the story how I told everyone else. He tells me how he feel about the situation and thinks that I should leave Frank, because I'm better than what he did, but I let him know that I still love him and couldn't.

"I can respect when you say you love him, but he shouldn't do you like this. You understand what I'm getting at? You are just too good for him."

"I know Jey, but you just don't understand. Can we just get off that please?"

"Yeah."

It was a long pause.

"You had to work today?" He tries to change the subject.

"No, I got to go tomorrow though. "

"Oh."

"My lip is still stinging."

"Has he ever hit you?"

"No, No. Hell no. If he ever put his hands on me he'll be a dead man. Aaron, Mieko, and Trill. Please." I lie, hiding it with a little laugh.

"You sure?"

"Yeah Jey."

"Alright."

Chapter 14

After me and NaNa talked I took her advice, I was going to step it up so that Frank wouldn't have time to think about another women. I picked up some cooking tips from him and got good at it. I cooked, cleaned, and made sure he had sex on the regular. With that, we brought in new stuff to the bedroom. We tried toys, lubes that gave off a different sensation, but it was one more thing that I wanted to try for him.

We were lying in the bed when I brought it up to him.

"Baby, I've been thinking about something we talked about before."

"What's that?"

I roll over on to my side and faced him. "You remember when we went to New York and you said something about having a threesome?"

"Yeah."

"Well I was thinking that we should try it together."

"You serious, baby?"

"Yes, I'm serious. I don't think it would hurt anything. It would bring more spice to our sex life."

"It would."

"But who would we get to have one with us?"

"I know the perfect person. I got this home girl that I've known for years, I know that she would be down with it."

"We should set it up for next Saturday."

When Saturday finally got here, I was nervous as hell. I thought about backing out of it, but I didn't go back on my word. Frank gave me a little information on the girl that would be coming over that we would be having this ménage with. Her name is Ariel, she's pretty, and that he'd known her since he came to Georgia.

Everything was planned to go down at Frank's house. I took a shower and made myself sexy. I was standing in the mirror when Frank walked in.

"You alright?"

"Yeah, I'm good."

"You sure? You haven't changed your mind have you?"

"No I haven't changed my mind. I'm kind of nervous though."

"For what? You looking sexy as hell. I'm not trying to lose you to her." He jokes.

"You know better than that."

"Come here."

I turn around and Frank tongues me down while grabbing my ass. He was making me so hot that it was about to go down before Ariel got there. Soon as I started to pull up his shirt, the doorbell rings.

"It looks like she's right on time." I laugh.

He bites his lips as he rolls his shirt back down. Before we go get the door he gives me a kiss on my forehead.

I go to the living room while Frank gets the door. When he gets back and I turn to see who this Ariel was, my jaw dropped.

"Baby, this is Ariel. Ariel this is..."

"Mm mm mm. Looks like we meet again," Ariel smiles.

"Yall know each other or something?" Frank was confused.

"You remember when I told you me and my friend went out, we went to Playa's Delight where she works."

"And your lady refused a dance from me, when I told her I would make it worth her wild." She walks over with a smirk on her face. "So how have you been lovely lady?"

"I've been good."

"Well, I'll fix some drinks and I'll be right back."

Frank leaves out and Ariel sits next to me on the couch.

"Small world huh?"

"Very."

"You can loosen up around me. I'm not going to bite, unless that's what you like." She smiles as she moves closer to me.

I fake a laughs. "How long have you known Frank?"

"Some years now." She kept her eye on me in a seductive manner. "So, is this your first time?"

"For what?"

"A threesome."

"Oh yeah."

"Being with a female?"

"This will be my first time." And last.

"I never though I'll see you again. I couldn't get your fine ass out of my head since the first time I saw you."

"Oh really." I say, knowing that she was running game like anyone else.

"Hell yeah." She moves closer to me. She didn't look like she was entertained by the questions I was asking her. Her eyes were scanning all over my body. "You look so sexy, I can't wait to taste that pussy." She comes closer, smelling and kissing my neck.

I move away.

"Don't run from me sexy." She runs her hand down my thigh. "I told you I'm not going to hurt you. I'm just here to pleasure you." She tries to pull at my shirt to see my breast, but I stop her.

"Here you go."

I jumped, because I didn't hear Frank come back in. Ariel laughs at me.

"How things been going Ariel?" He asks.

"Great. I'm glad you called me for this. You got you a real sexy something here Frank."

"I know." He kisses me as he sits down

We drank and made small talk. Frank went upstairs to make sure the room was set up right. I started feeling the liquor kicking in and knew I was feeling good, because Ariel started touching on me and this time I didn't move away.

"I want you so bad." She whispers into my ear.

I face her and she kisses me dead on. I didn't hold back, and she slowly slips her tongue into my mouth. She runs her hand up my shirt and start feeling on my breast through my bra.

I looked up and Frank was coming down the stairs watching us. He came and sat down and rubbed his dick through his pants. I turn my attention away from her and started kissing on Frank. Ariel reaches under us and pull up my shirt and start licking on my lower back, sending surges through my body, so I moan out.

"Yall ready to take this upstairs?" Frank asks.

We all get up and follow Frank to his room. I sit down on his bed and they both started feeling on me and kissing on me and pulling away my clothes.

She looks at Frank. "I want to taste your dick."▢

They both remove their clothes and Frank goes over and turn down the lights. He comes over to the bed and lay down and Ariel positions her face over his large erection and begins to give him head.

I didn't want to be left out so I moved to him so he could taste my pussy.

"Bring that pussy here." He tells me.

168

"And face me." Ariel says.

I turn around and sit on Frank's face as Ariel continues to suck him and make noises.

Ariel comes up off of Frank. "I want a taste too. Ariel licks her lips."

"You cool with that." Frank asks.

"Yeah." I get off of him.

"You got a toy we can use too?" Ariel asks.

"Yeah." I reached into the draw and pulled out a bullet, rabbit vibrator, and a dildo.

"Come lay down on your back." Ariel instructs me.

I put the toys on the bed and lay down.

Ariel took her index finger and gently rubbed it up my pussy circling around my clit. She took two fingers and slowly put then into my wet box sending pleasure through my body.

I watch as Frank gets behind Ariel and enter her.

Ariel moans out and under her breath say, "Damn, I miss this dick," or at least that's what I made out.

Frank stares at me and I held it. It was like Ariel was the link between us and every stroke he gave her, I could feel it with each flicker of her tongue and the in and out motions of her fingers

Ariel gets the bullet and put it inside of me, sitting it right under my g spot and started licking my clit. I knew this would send me over board and I would cum quickly.

"Aah. Damn." I say.

"Mm. It fell good huh. I want you to nut baby."

Frank pumped inside her harder.

Ariel moans out, "Mmm. I'm bout to cum."

When she said that, my pussy started twitching and we both came. Frank pulls out of Ariel and I tell him to lie on the bed.

I tell Ariel, "I want you to lick your juices off MY dick," with enfaces on my.

Ariel did as I said, and then it was my turn. I straddled Frank, and slowly slid down letting myself adjust to him.

As I was on top of him riding, Ariel started rubbing up and down my body. She was playing with my titties and my clit.

Frank starts pumping underneath me. It was feeling so good to be caressed like this while getting fucked so good. I moan out and in the matter of seconds I came so hard, squirting on him.

Frank was still hamering away inside of me closing in on his orgasm, and he pulled out and Ariel caught all of his load in her mouth, not wasting any of it.

"Fuuccck," he groans out.

"Damn girl. You nasty." I smirk.

She giggles with a smile on her face.

We took a little break before we were at it again.

Chapter 15

Things had started to get better with me and Frank's relationship. We started spending more time together and going places like we did in the beginning of our relationship. I thought things were better until one night he proved me wrong.

We were laying down cuddling and his phone rings.

Frank looks at the caller ID. "I got to answer this. I'll be right back."

"Okay."

Frank gets up and goes into the bathroom. I roll over onto my stomach and focus my attention towards the bathroom door trying to listen.

"What up? Yeah. Yeah baby. I ain't forgot I'll be thru in a min. Bye." He ended the call.

"Who was that baby?"

"That was business. So I gotta be out."

I look at the clock. "At two thirty in the morning?"

"Yeah."

"I though you was going to spend the night here."

"Yeah, but business came up. I ain't trying to put business over you, but I got to do what I got to do," He says as he puts his shirt back on.

I roll my eyes.

He finish putting his clothes on, and I walk him to the door.

"I guess I'll see you later."

"Okay," I reach up to him and give him a kiss. "Be careful."

"I will."

"See ya later." He walks off to his car.

I lock the door behind him and I go get back in bed. I couldn't go right to sleep, because I knew what Frank was getting ready to go do. I could of stopped him and confronted him right then, but couldn't. I lay in bed and cried myself to sleep.

I woke a few hours later at eight and called Frank.

"Hello?" he sounded as if I had woke him up.

"Hey baby. Sorry I woke you."

"You good. What's up?"

"I was calling to see if you were ok."

"I'm good."

172

A female voice says, "Baby. Come back to bed. You know I can't sleep when you ain't by my side."

"Who is that Frank?"

"Nobody baby."

I sit up in the bed. "I'm not stupid. I heard her voice. You were on the phone with her last night too."

Frank tries to explain. "Listen."

I cut him off. "Listen nothing. I'm tired of being played and lied to Frank. I just want you to be honest. Is it that hard."

"I'ma call you back when I wake up." He hangs up in my face.

I was getting so fed up with Frank and all the games he was playing.

I got dressed and started riding around town looking for Frank. Just so happen, I see his car parked at the Marriot hotel.

I walk inside the building and go up to the hotel clerk.

"Can I get the room number to Mr. Frank Johnson?"

"Relation to Mr. Johnson?" the clerk asks.

"I'm his wife Yolanda Johnson."

"He's in Room 222. Do you want me to let him know you're on your way up?"

"No. I want to surprise him." I smile.

"Ok."

I head over to the elevator.

"Excuse me ma'am."

I turn around.

"But there's an Ariel Johnson listed as his wife."

"Really," I say with anger in my voice.

The elevator beeped, I get inside, and rode to the right floor.

When I get off the elevator, I walked down three doors and there was the room. I knock on the door.

I could hear Frank through the door.

"It's probably housekeeping. I got this."

He comes to the door and opened up. He was indeed surprised to see me.

I pushed him out of the way looking for Ariel.

"Ariel. Where you at bitch?"

I look under the bed and in the closet. I then kick in the bathroom door. Ariel was standing there looking in the mirror putting on lipstick.

"You was looking for me?" She says sarcastically.

I charge at her and tackle her down to the floor.

"Ooh. I like to play ruff," Ariel says.

"You dirty bitch. I can't believe I trusted you just to be his friend.

I punch her in the face, but somehow she flips over on top of me.

"I eat them weak ass punches bitch, just like I ate you." She hits me and starts pulling my hair.

I find a way and kick her in the chest as hard as I could.

Ariel screams out in pain.

During this time, I didn't know where Frank was. He probably was sitting back laughing at our asses.

Ariel and I finally get back on our feet and start tussling till we fall in the Jacuzzi tub full of water.

We both were still fighting in the water. I got on top of her and held her face underwater.

Out of nowhere Frank reappears and takes my grip away from Ariel's face. She comes up from the water breathing hard, chest heaving.

"What the hell is wrong with you? You crazy or something?" Frank reprimands me.

I get out the water and stand right in front of Frank looking him straight in the face with a blank expression. With all my might, I punch him directly in his left eye. My fist hit like a brick to his face.

Running out the room, I head to the elevator. When it arrived, I got on and pressed the button for the lobby. When I got off I walked at a fast pace out of the hotel to my car, and I peel out to my house.

When I get home I cut off my cell phone, locked my front and back door, and lock all the windows. From the first incident, I made sure to never give Frank the key to my house back.

Thirty minutes later there was a knock on the door.

I peeped out of the blinds and it was Frank. His eye had turned black and a little puffy.

"Open up the door Applez. I know you're in there. I'm sorry," He pleas.

"Just go away. I don't have anything to say to you anymore."

"Come on babe. Just open the door." He hits the door with his fist.

"No!" I scream.

Frank walks away and get in to his car and drives off.

175

The house phone ring and it is Aaron.

"Hello." I answer.

"Hey. I called your cell phone and it went straight to voicemail."

"I turned it off. I didn't want to be bothered with. I Don't feel too good." I sit down.

"Hung over from last night?"

"No."

"Long night with ole buddie?"

"That's not it," I sniffle

"You need me to come over?"

"Yeah."

"I'll be over in a min sis."

"Ok."

We get off the phone.

Aaron comes over in the next ten minutes. When he came in the door I gave him a big hug.

"You alright?" Aaron asks.

"No. Can we sit down?"

We go sit on the couch.

"Come on. Talk to me." He put his arm around me and I lay my head on his chest like I use to do my dad.

"I know you warned me about this from day one, but I wasn't trying to hear it. I love Frank with all my heart, but I don't know what to do. I caught him cheating on me, and it was with somebody he introduced to me awhile back as a friend. I though nothing more of it though." I wiped the tears from my eyes. "I feel so dumb." I whisper, "The clues were there."

"I can't tell you no more than I've already have. As much as I want to get at him for putting you through stuff, it's your decision. I can't make up your mind for you, but I hope you make the right choice."

After he said that, we sat there in silence for a while.

"It's so easy to talk to you Aaron. You remind me so much of daddy. I really look up to you."

"I always promised him that I would look out for you and be there for you."

"You doing a great job of that. I know he is very proud of you. He had always liked you."

"Yeah

"Now Mieko on the other hand," I giggle. "You remember the first time he met him? He asked him what inner tube he floated here on."

We both laugh.

"Hell yeah."

Aaron stayed over for a while and kept me company as we talked liked we used to back in the day.

Chapter 16

A week went by and I still wouldn't talk to Frank, even after his endless attempts to contact me. I figured I had enough of time to cool down, and I that I didn't want to be with Frank anymore. I called him up and he answers.

"Hello."

"Hey."

"So, I guess you ready to talk?"

"Yeah, but I would rather us talk in person."

"Do you want me to come over there?"

"No, I'll come to you."

"I'll meet you over there."

I got dressed and went over to his house. When I got there, he was pulling up in the driveway. He gets out and I meet him at the front door.

He gives me a hug, but I let my arms stay at my sides.

"Can we go inside and talk?"

He unlocks the front door and we go inside and sit down.

He asks me, "How you doing?"

I shrug my shoulders.

He nods his head.

"Why couldn't you just tell me? I always told you to keep it real with me. From the beginning I told you I don't like surprises and I would like to know the hold truth than to be hurt by it later."

"I remember you saying that."

"Well why do you hurt me so much? All I want from you is to love me the same way I love you, because if you're not satisfied with me anymore, you should let me go."

"I do love you. I'm still interested in you and want to be with you."

"So why do you steady cheat on me?"

He doesn't respond, because he had no valid reason to cheat on me.

"I love you, but I don't know how I can keep going through this with you."

"Come on Applez. Don't start saying that."

"What else can I say? You don't know some nights I stay up crying, because I keep putting myself through this with you. Letting you treat me like this. Any time we get in an argument you put your hands on me.

For what reason? I'm not the one in the wrong." I start tearing up. "I got to go." I wipe my nose with my hand.

"Applez, don't go."

I stop at the door. "I have to."

Frank phone rings and he answers. I watch as his face turned sour. He hangs up the phone.

"What's wrong?" I say with great concern.

"They just rushed mama to the hospital. She just had a heart attack. I got to get to the hospital." He picks up his keys from the table and run to his car.

I close the front door and run behind him. "Wait, I'll go with you."

I hop inside the car with him and we rush over to the hospital.

When we get there we have to wait in the waiting room for a long time before the doctor comes out.

"Are you Frank Johnson?" The doctor walks up to Frank.

"Yeah," he answers.

"Your mom is stable, but we are going to run some more test before she can go home."

I ask, "Well, can we go back and see her now."

"Yes. Follow me."

We get up and follow the doctor to the room Frank's mom was in.

Frank walks in first. "Hey ma."

"Hey baby," Mama D say. "Hey there Ms. Yolanda."

"Hey Mama D."

"Ma, how you feel?"

180

"I'm okay baby, just feeling a little weak right now."

"You scared me."

"I scared myself too. Everything was going good. Me and the kids was out in the flower garden and I started feeling sharp pains in my chest. That's when I had Aaliyah to call 911."

"Where is Aaliyah and Tahji."

"Next door at Mae house. I asked her to watch them for me."

"After I leave here I'll go pick them up and bring them back to my house."

"Oh ok. Yall can have a seat."

We sit down and Frank takes the seat closes to her.

"How are you Yolanda? I haven't seen you in a while."

"I'm doing ok. I guess." I shrug my shoulders.

"You guess?"

"Just some personal issues, but it will be better."

"I hope so. Yall are too blessed to be stressed."

"I know, but things aren't always the way it seems."

Frank looks back at me and his mom looks at him. It remained silent for a while before Mama D spoke.

"It's starting to get late. Yall should go and get the kids. I'll be fine by myself tonight."

"I'll be back first thing in the morning mama."

"Ok baby."

Frank gets up so I follow his lead.

"Get better ma."

"I will."

He gives her a hug.

"See ya later Mama D. Hope you get better."

"Thanks baby."

Frank walks out the room.

"Hey Yolanda." She stops me. "The best advice I can give you is to walk away from it. Remember, I've been where you're at now. No matter how strong your love is, it seems never to be enough. And I know my son is just like his father. I never wanted our kids to follow in his footsteps."

I shake my head yeah and walk out the room to see Frank standing against the wall halfway down the hall.

"I thought you were right behind me."

"I was just telling your mom bye. That's all." I look up to him.

"Ok. You want me to drop you off to get your car?"

"No. I'll stay with you tonight."

We leave and go pick up his niece and nephew from the neighbor's house. When we got there, Aaliyah and Tahji came running out the house.

"Hey Uncle Frank," Tahji said hugging him at his knees.

"Hey Uncle Frank," Aaliyah said.

"You not going to give me a hug?" Frank asks her.

She hugs him and says hey to me. Tahji says hey too.

"Is Grandma going to be ok?"

"Yes, she's going to be ok. She has to stay in the hospital for a little while, so that she can get better."

Tahji asks, "Why can't she come home now?"

"She needs her rest."

"Ok."

"But tonight yall are going to going stay with Uncle Frank."

The both of them were excited.

When we got to Frank's house the kids was already sleep, so we put them to bed and we go to the den to relax.

"You look worried. Do you want to talk about it?"

He shakes his head yeah and I go over and sit behind him and I lay his head on my chest.

"It's really getting to me that ma is in the hospital. I know the doctors say that she will be alright, but I don't like to see her like that."

"I know how you feel."

"Out of all my life, I never remember seeing my mom sick, a cold or anything. So to see her in the hospital ..." he stops talking.

I start rubbing his hair.

"Everything gonna be alright. Mama D is a strong lady. See I'll bounce back."

"I know, but if I was to ever lose her, my life wouldn't be the same. I don't know how you did."

"Me either. First it was my dad, then my boyfriend, then my mom. It hurt so bad, but I had to stay strong, especially when my dad died. I saw most of it happen, except them actually shooting him. I saw the two dudes dressed in all black walk his way and pull out their guns. I ran from the window downstairs, but before I got all the way down them I heard the guns go off."

"I always regretted not yelling or something to warn him that they were behind him. He probably would have had time to shoot back, but it's like I couldn't say anything."

We both remained quiet.

Frank and I hadn't bonded in quite a while, and this was refreshing for me.

The next morning, I wake up to the sound of children in the room and I almost didn't know where I was at.

Frank and I had fallen asleep on the couch.

"Good morning Ms. Applez." Aaliyah says while running after her brother Tahji around the table.

"Good morning. Stop running, before yall hurt yall selves. How long have yall been up?"

"Just a little while." Aaliyah says.

"Uh huh. We brushed our teeth and everything. See." He comes over to me showing me his teeth.

I smile. "That's great."

"Ms. Applez. I'm hungry."

"Ok." Frank was still asleep on me as I try to sit up. "We will fix yall something for breakfast, when Uncle Frank wakes up."

"Frank baby. Wake up."

He doesn't say anything, so I kiss the top his head and rub his chest.

"Wake up baby."

He finally stretches back and opens his eyes.

"Good morning." I say.

"Good morning." He sits up.

Aaliyah and Tahji both tell him Good Morning.

I say in my cutest little kid voice, "Uncle Frank, we are hungry."

He laughs. "Okay I will fix breakfast soon as I wash up and get dressed."

"I need to too."

"I want yall to play nice down here while we go upstairs. That means no running around. No messing with nothing you got no business with. Understood?"

"Understood." Aaliyah and Tahji replies.

We both go upstairs and take quick shower together and get dressed. We come back down stairs to the kids watching cartoons.

"Yall ready for Uncle Frank's special French toast sticks?"

"Yeah," they both jump for joy.

All of us went into the kitchen and helped Frank make the French toast sticks. With them, we had sliced strawberries and orange juice.

I give Frank a kiss on the cheek. "Breakfast was great baby."

"Thank you." He returns my kiss to my forehead. "Is everybody ready to go see Mama?"

We go back to the hospital to visit Frank's mom, they planned to keep her over the next few days. After she got better, Aaliyah and Tahji went back to stay with her. Frank would go over to visit her more often to make sure that she was doing good.

Chapter 17

Things between me and Frank were going ok. Aaron was having a birthday party and he decided to come with me.

"Who Aaron think he is, Diddy or something with this all white party?"

"Don't do my brother. I know this party is going to be turnt up though. Aaron use to throw the best parties back when we were in High School, hopefully he still got it."

"You looking fine though baby." He says while looking at me through the mirror as he was brushing his hair.

I wore some white high waist slim legged pants with a white tuxedo styled blazer with black trim on the collar and my breast were sitting up looking good. I paired my outfit with some black single sole heels and a Chanel bag that Frank got me. My makeup was very neutral, but I had a bold red lip. I got my nails and hair done earlier that day. My hair was simple with a part in the middle and I had some extensions added into it.

"Thank you. You look good too."

Frank had on some white pants and a white blazer that only had three buttons that exposed his black button up shirt underneath. He also had some red Louis Vuitton loafers. He was looking real GQ status.

"Maybe too good." I smile. "All in that mirror like you trying to impress somebody."

"Whenever I go out I always got to make a statement." He put the brush down on the counter. "I swear if we ain't had to go nowhere, I would fuck you right now as good as you looking."

"Well I guess you like that I chose this look over wearing a dress."

"Yeah, I already know you look good in a dress, but you looking sexy as hell in this right now." He pulled me closer to him and kissed me.

"Come on baby before you mess up my lip stick." I rub my thumb across his lips removing the little bit that stained his lips from the kiss.

"I'll wait to do that later then." He smiled at me. "Let's get out of here."

We get into Frank's car and drive down to the venue that Aaron was having his birthday party at. The parking lot was already full of cars and some people outside.

Frank and I were on the VIP list, so we were treated with special care skipping the line that was outside of people trying to get in.

Inside, I spotted NaNa. Frank said he was going to mingle while me and NaNa talked.

"Girl you looking too good. I like this little fit you got on."

Spinning around I showed off my outfit. "Thank you. I decided to wear this, because I wanted to make a statement."

"Well that you did. I saw Frank come in looking like he come straight off GQ cover."

"Yeah, my baby looking good huh?"

"Mhm. Both of your boo's looking good tonight."

"What you talking about?"

"Jeremy is here."

I was surprised, because he didn't let me know that he was coming to town like he normally did. "He didn't even let me know that he was coming."

"That's probably because he didn't come alone." She nodded and pointed in the direction of Jeremy and his girlfriend. "She's cute."

Jealousy was the feeling that I was feeling at the moment. Bianca was indeed cute. She wore her hair in a short pixie cut that really fit her face. She and I looked to be the same height.

"Looks like they are headed this way." NaNa stated.

"Hey Yolanda this is Bianca. Bianca this is my friend Yolanda. You've already met Natosha"

"Hey." She waved not really interested in getting to know me.

"Jeremy has told me about you." I try to make conversation.

"Funny thing is he never mentioned you." She directed all of her attention to Jeremy. The comment she made was a blow to the both us. "I'm about to get me a drink." She says before she walks away to the bar.

"Well." I say.

"You are a better woman than me, because that little comment would of got her ass checked." NaNa says.

"I'm sorry about that." Jeremy apologizes for the actions of his girlfriend.

"No offense taken. If I knew my man had a female friend as fine as me, I would be mad too." I try to make light of the situation. "I see you wasn't going to tell me you were coming to town."

"I already told you how she is, so she would have been jumping to conclusions to hear us on the phone."

"I bet she got a lot to jump to now though." NaNa laughs.

"You looking nice tonight." I look him up and down.

"Not as good as you though."

"Well we know that."

We were all smiling and laughing when NaNa whispered to me, "Here comes Frank," then walks off.

"NaNa." I call to her so she wouldn't leave me alone with Jeremy with Frank coming over, but she kept going and spoke to Frank as they bypassed each other.

"Hey baby, I don't think I've formally introduced you two." He wraps his arm around my waist pulling me in to him. "Frank this is my friend Jeremy. Jeremy this is Frank."

"Her boyfriend Frank." He tightens his arm around my waist.

Jeremy nods his head, not phased by Frank's passive aggressiveness.

Frank's phone goes off. "I'll be right back bae." He kisses me on the neck and whispers in my ear, "Don't go anywhere."

"Okay." I respond.

He walks away from us and outside to answer the call. I look from the door to Jeremy.

"Ya boy seems threatened or something, how he cuffing on you like I was going take you away from him."

"Nothing serious. All yall dudes are like that when another guy is around your girl."

"Not me. I got confidence in myself that I don't have to play the jealous role."

"Your girl doesn't look like she cared too much to get to know me."

"I told you how she is."

"The jealous type huh?" I laugh.

"Yeah. She is probably somewhere pouting right now.

"I don't know what to say about her."

"Me either."

I look over to the door and Frank was headed back over. When he saw that I was still talking to Jeremy his expression changed to anger.

"Jey, I'll be right back."

I hurry up and walk over to Frank before he could make it to Jeremy and embarrass me. "Is everything ok?" I was referring to the phone call.

"What was you still doing over there with him?"

"You told me to stay right there and I did."

"But I ain't tell you to be smiling up in his face and shit."

"Frank, he is just a friend. Nothing to worry about."

"Get your shit, because I'm ready to leave."

"For what? We just got here."

He lowers his voice. "Like I said, get your shit, because I'm ready to go."

I saw the anger in Frank's face, so instead of fighting the situation I complied with what he said. "I'm about to tell Aaron I'm about to go."

I go over to Aaron. "Hey A. Sorry to come and go, but something came up and me and Frank are about to head out."

"Yall just got here, everything straight?"

"Yeah, but anyway, I hope you have a great birthday. Sorry I couldn't stay longer." I hug him and give him a kiss on the cheek.

"Alright. If you need, you can call me."

I shake my head. I go back over to Frank and he grabbed my arm and led me out the door to the car.

"What were you thinking?" He asks me.

"What do you mean?"

"I go inside and you're smiling up in ole buddy face. Flirting and shit."

"I was not flirting with him."

"Quit your bullshit lies. I know what you were doing."

"I'm telling you the truth, it was nothing like that. We were just talking."

"Ok. We'll see."

Nothing else was said from there until we got back to his place. He had me beyond mad, but I kept everything in to myself, because I wanted the night to go by smoothly, but it didn't.

"Get your lying ass in the house," he told me as he opened the door.

I walk pass him and he pushes me and I turn and look back at him.

"What?" He said in a threatening tone.

I just continued to walk in the house.

He pushes me again.

"Quit Frank."

"What you going to do about it if I don't. You love when other people pushing up on you, but not your man."

"Why do we always have to argue?"

"I'm not arguing with you. I just want you to tell the truth."

"And that's what I've been doing. Telling you the truth."

"No you're not. I know you and him got something going on."

I huff. "Ok Frank if you want me to, I'll tell you he was flirting with me just to make you happy I will. We was flirting. But that is not what happened ok." I walk toward the staircase, but is pulled back from Frank.

"Where you going?"

"Leave me alone. You know what," I pause, "I'm about to leave, that's what I'm about to do."

"You ain't going nowhere."

"Yes I am. Matter of fact I'm going back to my best friend's party." I head to the door.

"Bitch you ain't going no where."

"What in the hell you just call me?" I put my hands on my hips and waited for his response.

"Bitch."

I slap him in the face, "And you had the audacity to repeat yourself."

Why did I do that? Frank punched me in my face. The force from the hit knocked me up against the wall, and I hit the floor like a ton of bricks.

Standing over me breathing hard, he spat on me.

I felt my jaw to see if it was broken and it wasn't. I gathered all my strength together and stand up. "I get it."

Frank turns around surprised that I was up.

"I get it. You trying your best to bring me down as low as you are. I'm tired of this shit." I walk out the door and he follows out behind me.

"Baby, I'm sorry. I didn't mean to."

"You never mean to, but yet you still do." I wipe away the blood that was trickling down from my lip.

"I'm sorry. I can't stand the thought of you with someone else. It just hurt me to see you with another man."

"It hurt you? We wasn't even doing anything, so if that hurt you, what do you think I feel when I catch you cheating on me? I be so mad, but I still run back to you, because I love you and have hope that you won't do it again. Time after time you have proved me wrong."

"Baby." He tries to touch me.

"Don't touch me Frank."

He tries again and I don't stop him. "I need you Yolanda, and I don't want you to leave me. I love you so much. I'm sorry that I do the things I do to hurt you. Baby, please come inside. I promise if you want to leave in the morning, I will take you home. Just come inside and cool down." He kissed me on the forehead. He released his arms from around me and walked back into the house.

Even if I wanted to leave at that moment, I couldn't because my car was at my house and Frank would have been my only means of transportation anywhere.

I walk back to the house and lock the door behind me. I walked up the stairs to Frank's room and lay down. He came in and lay behind me holding me. Crying silently is how I fell asleep that night.

A couple months had gone by and I hadn't seen my period. The first month I racked it up to stress being the reason why it didn't come, but after the second month I knew there had to be another reason.

While I was out, I had picked up a pregnancy test at the drug store and hurried home to take it. The wait seemed like hours and when the timer went off on my phone for the test being done, I didn't know what the results would be.

I went to the room where Frank was at and stood there in the middle of the bedroom doorway. "Baby," I look up from the pregnancy test, "I'm pregnant."

He walked over to me and dropped down to his knees and put his head to my belly and kissed it. I didn't know how he would feel at first, because we never really talked about having kids, but this gave me the perfect conformation. Coming to his feet he kisses me on the lips and then the forehead.

"So you are happy?"

"Yes, I am happy. Why does that seem to surprise you?"

"I just never," I shook my head, "We never really talked about having kids. Of course I know you love them, by seeing how you are with Aaliyah and Tahji, but I didn't know if you wanted any of your own."

"I've always wanted kids, just never found the person that I wanted to have kids with."

"Did you plan on us having kids?"

"Eventually yeah, but I'm happy."

After the news, Frank stepped it up a little bit, but for a short while. The arguing still remained and it got back to the point where he started hitting on me again.

"You said you were going to change Frank, but you still out here doing the same thing. I'm tired of worrying about you at night. I fear that you might get killed out in them streets, and I need you now more than anything."

"Whatever Yolanda. You don't have to worry about that, because I'm untouchable in these streets, and if I so happen to get killed, I got a stash that can support you and our baby for a long time."

"I don't wanna hear that extra shit Frank. You need to quit thinking about you and start thinking about us. It's more to a family than financial support. I need you there physically and emotionally."

Frank phone goes off.

"And there that damn phone goes again. I know you still out there fucking other females."

"You don't know shit. I ain't fucking nobody."

"You gotta be fucking somebody, because you ain't been fucking me like you use to."

"I've been busy." He walks out the room to the hallway.

"Bullshit. You can quit lying Frank. I know your motives."

"You don't know shit and don't call me a liar."

I shake my head. "Why you get mad when I speak the truth? If I was out here doing what you doing, you wouldn't like it either. Now bet that. Put a grand on that shit."

He slapped me so hard I fell into the wall and I couldn't catch my balance before I tumbled down the stairs. It was a bad pain in my stomach and I knew it wasn't good news. Frank came running down the stairs after he realized what he had done and what could be the results of what he had just did.

"Baby I'm sorry. I didn't mean to. Are you alright?"

"No. It feels like something ripped in my body."

"I got to get you to the hospital." He picked me up and toted me to the front door and he picked up his keys on the way out.

He drove in a hurry to the hospital

"What happened?"

I looked at Frank and back at her. "I got dizzy and lost my balance and fell down the stairs. Now I have bad pains in stomach. I just found out I was pregnant. I hope there's nothing wrong with my baby."

After they run some test and do an ultrasound, the nurse and doctor comes back into the room.

"Ms. Smith, I'm sorry, but you lost the baby."

I turned my head to the window and tears flooded from eyes without a sound. I knew I had lost our baby, and Frank was the cause, and he knew it too.

"Are you ok Ms. Smith." The nurse asked.

I shook my head, but didn't say anything.

"Can we have some time alone?" Frank asked the doctor and the nurse.

They walk out of the room and Frank comes over to me and touches my leg. "Baby?" I move it. "Baby, I'm sorry. I didn't mean to."

"You never mean to."

He sits down on the edge of the bed where I had my back turned to him.

"I thought you loved me."

"I do love you."

"Well why you keep putting your hands on me?" He couldn't say anything. "That was our child. If you loved me you wouldn't put your hands on me, especially knowing that I was carrying your seed."

Frank didn't say anything. He just stood up.

"Can I please be alone for a few?"

He walked out of the hospital room without saying anything, and I cried. I hadn't cried that hard since my mom died. Even though I was only three months I had grown attached to my child. I wanted to see someone that belong to me grow up to be a great man or woman, and I would love them unconditionally and they love me just the same.

I hadn't even told Aaron, NaNa, and the guys I was pregnant, and now I would have to find some way to tell them I had a miscarriage.

When I got home the living room was filled with bouquets of roses and white lilies. It made me smile, but it didn't make up the fact for what Frank did. I saw my voicemail blinking on my house phone and I knew when I turned on my cell phone calls and messages were going to come.

There were calls from NaNa, Jeremy, Aaron, and even Miami.

'What's up Applez? I've been trying to get in touch with you all night. What's up with you? Hit ya bro back.' –Aaron

'Hey girl. I was wondering did you wanna go out to eat with me tomorrow. Call me back and let me know.' – Miami

Jerermy

-Appppppppppplllllllleeeeeeeeeeeeezzzzzzzzzzzzz lol
-Oh so we not responding back
-You alright? Get at me when you get this
-Hit me up asap

'Damn, a bitch ain't even answering the phone. Damn I see how we do. I come by your house and you ain't even there and you ain't tell me if you were going out of town. Mm.'

After I got done reading the rest of the messages I go into my room and there were rose peddle on my bed and a note in an envelope.

Baby, I know I may not show it at times, but I do love you from the bottom of my heart. I'm sorry about everything I've done to you. I'm sorry about being the cause of you losing our child. I feel your hurt, because our baby was a part of me too. I promise to be there and show you that I want to make it better. Please forgive me.

Frank

I went to the bathroom to take a bath. I sat in there for almost an hour, reflecting on what had recently happened in my life and how I was going to move on from it. After I finally got out, I went to the closet to find something to put on, and it was filled with new clothes and shoes.

It was a nice gesture, but if Frank really knew me, he would know that the material things didn't mean anything to me. I closed back the doors and went to the dresser and found a pair of shorts and a t-shirt to put on.

My phone started ringing and it was Aaron.
"Hey."
"What up? I've been hitting you up."
"Nothing. I'm just getting back home."

"Me and Mieko bout to come through."

"Ok."

"Aiight. I'll be there in five."

I sat there flipping through the channels on the TV trying to find something to watch, but I couldn't find anything, so I just left it on a movie that was playing.

Ten minutes later there was a knock at the door and it was Aaron and Mieko. I went and answered it.

"Hey." I said before turning around and letting them inside.

"Damn what's up with all these flowers?" Mieko says as they come in the house.

"Frank sent them to me."

"For what, an anniversary or something?" Aaron says.

"I was in the hospital all yesterday till this morning."

"And you didn't tell us?" Aaron says.

"Why you was in there?" Mieko asks

"I had got dizzy and fell down the steps at Frank's house."

"And that make you have to stay at the hospital overnight?" Mieko was confused.

"Um, the reason I had to stay is because not long after I fell I started having bad abdominal pains, so Frank rushed me to the hospital, and I found out I had a miscarriage."

"A miscarriage? Aaron says.

"Yes a miscarriage."

"Did you know you were pregnant?"

"Yeah. I found out when I was two months. I would have been three months Friday."

"And when were you going to tell us?"

"I didn't know how to tell yall. I know how yall feel about Frank, so I was trying to figure out the best way to tell you."

Aaron shook his head in an 'I can't believe it' way. "So why he ain't here now?"

"I wanted to be alone for a few hours."

They stayed for a while till I told them that I was tired and wanted to go rest for a while. I decided to call Jeremy since I owed him a call back.

"So look who decides to finally call somebody back."

"Hey Jey."

"Why you ain't been hitting me up?"

"I've been going through a lot."

"A lot like what?"

"Personal things between me and Frank."

"Oh." He says nonchalantly.

"I had to go to the Emergency Room yesterday. I got out this morning."

"Why? What was wrong?"

"When I was at Frank house I was upstairs and got dizzy and fell all the way down the stairs. I was having bad stomach pain, so he rushed me to the hospital."

"You alright though, right?" He sounded very concerned.

"I guess so. When I got there I found out I had a miscarriage."

"You had a miscarriage? You were pregnant?"

"Yeah. I would have been three months this Friday. I just found out last month, and I didn't know how to tell any of yall, because I know how yall feel about Frank, but I was going to tell you. I just didn't expect for it to happen this way."

"I'm sorry to hear that. How you feel though, about having the miscarriage and all?"

"It hurts, because even though I didn't know for very long I got attached to the fact that I was having a child. Health wise I am ok though."

"I wish I was there to be by your side through this."

"I'll be ok."

"I just wanna be there in person, so you can talk to me and I be that shoulder you could cry on if you need too."

"Thank you Jeremy."

"That's what I'm here for."

"What you up to anyhow?"

"In class."

"In class Jay! You didn't have to answer, you could of text me back."

"I stepped out. It's almost the end of class anyway."

There was a brief silence between the both of until Jeremy spoke again. "Applez, I'ma be there for you as soon as I can, alright?"

"You don't have to rush here for me. I'll be alright."

"I want to though."

"I'm really glad that you're my friend, because you are always there for me no matter what."

"That's what a real friend is supposed to do."

Frank comes back in a few hours and I was lying in bed. He got in bed behind me and wrapped his body around me.

"I love you baby and I'm sorry again."

I turned over to face him. "I love you too." I give him a kiss on the lips.

"How you feel?"

I shrug my shoulders. "Tired. I need to take my medicine in a few."

"You want me to cook you something, so you can eat with it?"

"That would be nice."

"What do you want to eat?"

"Maybe a sandwich or something."

Chapter 18

Time had gone by and I was feeling better, so I went over to Aaron's place to pay him a visit. "Knock, knock." I say as I knock on his door. Moments later Aaron came to the door.

"What up Applez?" He moves out of the way and let me come inside.

"Nothing much just wanted to come through and see you.

We sat down and Aaron got right to it.

"I already know what's up with you and Frank, and I know you didn't get dizzy and fall down no stairs."

"Aaron I..."

"Please don't come up with some bullshit excuse. You don't have to lie to me. I've been doing like you told me and been staying out of your business, but I know the truth, and I wouldn't be doing what your dad told me to if I didn't look out for you." I didn't say anything as Aaron continued. "I've seen you change Applez. The old you would never put up with what's going on. A couple of people told me what happened outside at the party between you two."

"It was just a little argument."

"I heard about Frank's ex Latesha. They said Frank use to beat the shit out of her. She would fight back, but it didn't work. She wouldn't leave him, because she was so in love with him, just like you make out to be. You know where she at now?"

"No."

"She's dead. He beat her so bad that she had internal bleeding and the doctors couldn't stop it. The only reason he ain't locked up now is because when she was at the hospital she said she had got jumped by these girls that disliked her."

I looked at him in his eyes.

"I bet he never even told you about that though. I swear Applez, I'm not going to sit here and watch you go through the same thing. I know it's more to what you be telling us. You know you can always talk to me."

I couldn't say anything after that.

As usual things didn't change with Frank we continued to argue off and on about any and everything. It got to the point where I was fed up with it all.

"Are you listening to me? Are you listening?"▢

"Yeah I hear you Frank. You yelling loud enough."

"Well act like it then."

"What the hell is your problem? You need to gone with that bullshit."

Frank pushed me full force into the wall.

"Who the hell you talking to like that."

I get real calm. "Alright Frank. I don't know what my problem was with yelling back at you. I always deserve what is coming for me right?"

I get my stuff together as Frank is still talking.

"What the hell are you doing?"

"I'm going home. I got to go to work in the morning."

"So you just going to leave in the middle of me talking to you."

I open up his front door. "Bye Frank. I'm done." I close the door behind me and get into my car and go home.

On the drive home Frank was blowing my phone up, but I didn't answer. Since I figure he would try to come by I went over to NaNa's to see what she was up to, after I left there I decided to go back home.

I stopped by the liquor store to get something to get me something to drink. When I got out the car when I got home, I turn around to hear a car pulling up in my driveway. It was Jeremy.

He gets out the car. "I guess I came just in time." He saw the alcohol I had just bought from the store.

"What you doing here?"

"No hey, how you doing?"

"I'm sorry Jey. I didn't mean to come off that way." I continued to walk to the house and I unlocked the door and we went inside.

"You alright?"

"Yeah I'm ok."

"No you're not. I know when something's wrong with you."

"I broke up with Frank."

Jeremy sat down next to me on the sofa and I don't know why, but I started bawling out tears. Everything seemed to hit me at that moment and I couldn't control the tears.

He laid my head onto his shoulder. Not even saying anything, the way he was caressing me was comforting and it helped me calm down.

"What happened?"

"I caught him cheating on me a few days ago with someone I thought was only his friend. I don't know how I could be so stupid to believe that."

"That's the best thing you could have done. You deserve better anyway."

"I know."

Jeremy and I start drinking and talk about the problems that we both were going through and before we knew it, we both started to feel good.

"Come to bed with me Jey."

"You sure?"

"Yeah I'm sure." I stood up and pulled Jeremy to a standing position. He followed me to the room. I took off my clothes down to my bra and panties.

"What are you doing?"

I smile. "I'm just changing into some shorts and a tank top. Chill."

He laughs and sits on the foot of the bed.

"You can take off your pants and shirt if you want to."

Jeremy undressed and laid on his side facing me. What I did next evidently surprised him. I put my leg around his body and came as close as possible to him.

"Applez I know if we hadn't been drinking, we wouldn't be doing this."

"Jey, I know exactly what I'm doing, and it's not because I had anything to drink or because I'm using you as a rebound from Frank. I want this right now. Do you?"

"Yeah, I do."

Moving my face closer to his, I closed my eyes and kissed Jeremy. I wanted this moment so bad and this breakup with Frank was the perfect excuse to go ahead and do so. I explored his mouth with my tongue and he did the same.

Jeremy gripped on my butt pulling me closer to him. I took my hand and put it down his shorts to caress his growing erection. He stopped kissing me and looked down at what I was doing and looked back to me. I shook my head yeah, because I knew he was still questioning my actions.

I pushed Jeremy onto his back with my body and sat on top of him and continued kissing him and started grinding on top of him feeling his full on erection pressing against me through his shorts.

"I want you so bad Applez. I need you."

"I need you too."

He reaches behind me and unhooks my bra and puts it over to the side. He sits up and licks and sucks on my breast driving me insane. I lean over and look in my draw for a rubber. After Jeremy takes off his shorts he puts it on and I position myself over him to prepare for my ride.

I slowly slide down and Jeremy fit my body like it was made for him. He let out a groan as I started riding.

I found my perfect rhythm and he started bucking underneath me.

"Damn Applez."

We were laying there in silence, until I spoke.

"I'm sorry Jey."

"For what?"

"For making you cheat on your girlfriend."

He turns to face me. "Applez, you have nothing to be sorry for. I wanted this too." He caresses my face. "I don't love her anymore, besides I was always in love with you." He pauses. "Me and her decided to take a break, but I'm ready to officially break it off with her."

"Don't do that because of me."

"I'm doing it because I want to. I rather live my life with the person I love and that I know loves me back than someone who takes everything I do for granted."

"I love you too Jeremy." I kissed him and laid my head on his shoulder and fell asleep.

Chapter 19

A week and a half go by and I was purposely avoiding Frank. I wouldn't answer his calls and wouldn't go by his house. He showed up to my house.

"Why you ain't been answering my calls?"

"I've been busy." I flip the page of a new book that I was reading by my favorite author Sierra Denise.

"Why you ain't call back?"

"I don't know." I shrug my shoulders.

"Probably the same reason you keep making excuses for not coming over to my house. Who you fucking?"

"What?" I look up from my book.

He gets loud. "Who else besides me you fucking?"

"You trippin." I continue reading trying to ignore him.

"You lying ass bitch."

I stand up in front of him. "Hold on, nobody about to call me out of my name. Just because you fucking all these other hoes out here don't mean I'm out here fucking nobody else. Even though I know you messed with them other girls, I was still sticking to you side, but I see you don't care about none of that shit. And every time you hit me, I run back to you like a little fool trying to prove my love to you. If you really love me, you wouldn't do what you did to me."

I whisper under my breath. "I knew I should have never got involved with you in the first place." I walk away a little bit, but he grabs me by the arm and pulls me to him.

"What? What was that you just said? You shouldn't have got involved with me?"

"Let go of me Frank." I try to shake loose, but his grip got tighter. "Stop." I scream out.

He back hands me and I hit the couch. He just went off and started punching me all over me. He tried hitting me in my face, but I kept it blocked, but he eventually got me.

He left me there beaten up. I couldn't even move. I stayed there on my couch for a good three hours. I finally get up and make it to my bathroom. I still had a faded black from the week before. I had bruises on my arms, back and one big one on my thigh. I took a deep breath and put on some make up around my eye.

I hadn't really talked to any of my friends like that in the past week. The pain and stress of dealing with Frank I couldn't take anymore and I need to let someone know.

I sit and cried again about everything that has been going on in my life between me and Frank. I cried for my mom and dad.

My phone ringed and it was Jeremy.

I wipe my eyes. "Hey Jey."

"Me and Bianca just had a big fight and I'm officially leaving her. I'm on my way down there right now. I shouldn't have even moved in with her stupid ass."

"What? She kicked you out?"

"Yeah, and this is the best opportunity for moving back. I'm through with her. I'm headed down there now."

"What time you think you going to be here?"

"I'm about thirty minutes away."

"Could you come by after you get back?"

"Yeah I'll be there."

I hang up, and flip my hair out of my face. "I need to get myself together." I slowly put on my jacket making sure not to cause pain to the new bruises he put on me earlier.

I needed to let Jeremy know everything that has been going on between me and Frank. It wasn't very long before he called and said that he was close.

There were knocks on the door, so I knew it was Jeremy. Soon as he saw me, he knew something was wrong with me.

"Who did this to you?"

"It's Frank." I take a deep breath. "He's been beating on me."

"What!" Jeremy was livid.

"He's been beating on me and just…" I bust out crying heavily and I put my face in my hands.

"I asked you. I asked was he hitting you, but you said no. Damn. You could have told me, and you know this."

I sit up. "I've been scared. I've wanted to tell someone, but I couldn't."

He moves closer to me. "I swear I'm going to fuck him up. A real man would never put his hands on a woman." He wraps his arms around me.

Jeremy asked me questions about everything that's been going on with me and Frank and I had been open and honest with him.

"I'm promise to never let him hurt you again." He kissed me and I took over the kiss, because at that moment I needed Jeremy.

"I don't want it to seem like I'm trying to take advantage of you while you feeling like this." He says in between kisses.

"No. I want this." I pause. "I want you." I look deep into his eyes.

We start back kissing and I lead him back to my room. I sit down at the foot of the bed and he sits next to me. I take off all of my clothes and lean back on the bed. He takes off his and gets on top of me kissing me.

He opens my legs, and ran his fingers down my wetness. A chill went through my body and I let out a sigh.

He puts his face down there and let his tongue slip inside of me, and started making nice long strokes across my clit. He became faster and harder with each flicker of his tongue making me scream out of control.

He returned his hands to my breast and squeezed firmly, and played with my nipples making them even harder. With his other hand he puts two fingers inside of me, while still licking on my clit. He found my spot and continues playing and I cum with such a force.

I pull him up to me and start kissing him tasting myself. I start stroking his large erection and I position him inside of me. He starts off slowly. Rubbing his hands across my face and kissing me on the neck. I sucked on his neck leaving a passion mark. I wrap my legs around him. He begins to pick up speed and I let out cries of pleasure and tears fell from the sides of my eyes, and Jeremy would wipe them away.

I could feel my orgasm coming and I reached my peak, as I erupted I felt him jerking inside of me as he came too.

We both have to catch our breath and he rolls over off of me.

"Come here."

I roll onto my stomach and lay on his arm.

"You deserve so much better than him, and you should know that."

"Yeah, I know. I'm going tomorrow to let him know that I never want anything to do with him again."

"You need me to come?" He asks.

"No, I got it."

"As beautiful as you are, I don't see how someone can do this to you. I know you know how I feel about you and everything. Yolanda I love you, and I always have.

I kiss him. "I love you too." I get on top of him, and continue making passionate love to him all night.

I wake up from a kiss on the cheek "Good morning." Jeremy says smiling.

"Morning." I couldn't help but smile. "I need to go take a shower."

"Can I get in with you?"

"Yeah." I get up and go to the bathroom and he follows me in.

When we get in the shower he washed my whole body from head to toe, and I do the same to him. After we get dried off we get dressed.

"I should be getting back to Trey's, but I'm going to be back over later."

"Ok, let me grab my keys." I get my keys.

"You sure you don't want me to go with you whenever you go?"

"Yeah. I'll be fine."

We leave out at the same time, but before I pulled off Jeremy gives me a kiss and tell me to call if I needed him.

On the way to Frank's house I call him and ask him could I meet him to his house so that we could talk about some things. He agreed.

When I got there, I take a deep breath and prepare myself before going inside. I go up and knock on the door. He soon comes to the door. "What's up?"

"Hey." I walked passed him into the living room and he closes the door and follows behind me and sit down on the couch. He pulls me into his lap, but I get up.

"What's this about?"

"I need to talk to you about something important."

"Go ahead." He sits back in the chair.

"I came to tell you that I can't put up with this anymore. I loved you so much that you didn't even understand. I can't keep going through this with you. I'm tired of you putting your hands on me every time we get in an argument. When our relationship first started off I felt like you was the one I wanted to spend my life with. You showed me a lot, but then it started getting *out of control*. I'm hurting more in the inside than the pain you causing on the out. I respect everything you do up until a certain extent. As much as I wanted this to be right, I know I could never do this again."

"So what you trying to say?" He sits up and I back up a little.

"I'm saying that I can't go on like this, and I don't want to be with you anymore. I don't want anything to do with you. Love shouldn't hurt like this."

He stands up and I back up some more. He shakes his head yeah. He puts his hand on his chin, and then he released his hand and hit me, knocking me to the ground. I try to get up, but he held me down chocking me.

"Stop." I manage to get out. I start kicking and try to hit him, but his strength over powered mine. He picks me up by my neck, still chocking me and throws me onto the couch and continues hitting me.

I kick him in the nuts and he open hand slaps me before falling back on the couch grabbing his self.

I run to the bathroom and locked the door behind me. I knew if I was to run to the door he would of come after me. I clean my face with a towel and had to think of a way out. Remembering how low his bathroom window is I jump out of it and run to my car and speed off to Aaron's house.

When I get there I burst through the door, and Aaron and Mieko was in the living room and they jumped up from their seats.

"What the fuck happened?" Aaron yells.

"It's Frank. Frank has been beating me."

Mieko ask, "How long this been goin on?" He puts his arms around me.

"After the first time that I caught him cheating on me."

Mieko takes me to the couch.

"Why you haven't told anyone? Damn Applez."

"I don't know. I was scared."

"Fuck this, I'm about to kill this nigga." Aaron was angry.

"You don't know Frank like I know him. He is dangerous."

He gets his phone and start dialing a number.

"Who you calling?" I ask.

"Trill, we about to ride on this nigga Frank. I'll explain when we get you."

They leave and I lock up the door. I call Jeremy and let him know and he comes over.

"I should of went with you." He wraps his arms around me. "I should of went." He kisses me on the forehead.

"Can we sit down?"

We walk over to the chair.

"I can't believe I let this get to this point. I feel so stupid for letting this happen. I tried fighting back, but it didn't work. It only added fuel to the fire."

"You're not stupid, you just though you were in love. You wanted him to replace the spot in your life where you were missing your dad."

"All the shit I done been through, I thought I could trust him. In the beginning we were like one, but that just turned in a heartbeat. My life is so fucked up."

"But it'll get better. Believe me it will."

My phone rings and it is Frank, but I let it ring. He leaves a message saying that I better not do anything stupid and that was it.

"He is crazy."

"What?"

"He said I better not do anything stupid. I hope Aaron nen get him."

A few minutes later there is some knocks at the door.

"Girl it's me NaNa."

I get up and open the door for NaNa.

"Oh my god girl." She said soon as I let her in. "Mieko called and told me everything, and told me to come over to see about you. You ok girl?"

"Yeah. I'm just in pain."

"You want me to take you to the emergency room."

218

"No, I'll be fine."

"I told you to let me know anything ever happened to you like this."

"I know NaNa. I was scared, and now I'm tired of tell this story, because it's going to make me cry again."

"Ok. Do you need anything?"

"Yeah. Can you get me some ice."

"Yeah."

I lean up against Jeremy and he puts his arm around me. NaNa comes back with the ice and Jeremy rubs it across my bruises.

It was late that night when Mieko, Aaron and Trill got back. They said they couldn't find him anywhere. They even went to the spot where he go and catch up with Boob and Stretch, they still couldn't find him. They went all over the city.

I figured that Frank had probably left town, but it still had me scared that he was still out there and could possibly try to hurt me again. Jeremy stayed with me every day, because I was scared to be alone. Even Aaron, Mieko, and Trill kept up with me. I was a wreck for the next days. I even went as far as quitting my job because I didn't want him to show up there.

Jeremy stayed with Trey for the time being, but spent most of his time over here. He chose to start school down here, so he had to go out to the school and check on some paper work.

"I'll be back later baby. I need to go out to the school and check on my transfer papers."

"Ok baby."

"You going to be alright without me?"

"Yeah, I'm straight. I need to run to the store real quick and pick up some things anyway."

"Alright."

I walk with him to the door and give him a kiss on his way out.

"I love you."

"I love you too," he responds.

I watch him drive off.

I go to the room and get my purse before I leave out the door. I go down to the grocery store to pick up a few things and come back. I turn off the car get out and out and mash the lock. Then I walk to the door and look for the key to the house.

"Yolanda. Let me talk to you real quick."

I turn around and I see Frank walking my way. I try to put the key in the hole, and unlock the door, but before I could turn the knob he grabs my arm.

"Where you trying to go?"

"Stop. Let me go." I yell.

He pushes me inside and locks the door behind him.

"I'm tired of your shit Frank. You need to leave my house or I'm going to call the police on you."

"I see how you be having ole buddy coming in and out of here all the time and wasn't you thee one who said wasn't nothing going on between you too."

I say nothing.

"What? You been fucking him? Was he better than me?" He looks me up and down. "Probably not." He laughed.

"What do you want?"

220

"I need a reason to be over here now. You wasn't asking that when you was getting this good dick, and spending my money."

"I told you I don't want you here. Can you just go…"He puts his hands around my throat. "Frank." I gasp for air.

"You think you Mrs. Badass now? Huh?"

"Fuck you Frank?" I try to shake loose.

"You want me to let go?" He lets me go and I put my hand to my throat where he was chocking me. Frank acts as if he was going to walk away, but turns around and slaps me so hard that I let out a scream. "Talk that big shit now."

Franks starts going off on me with blows all over my body. He grabbed me by arms and dragged me towards the bedroom kicking and screaming. I was hoping to god that someone one would hear my cries.

He then throws me onto the bed. "I'm going to give you something to scream about.

"Please don't do this Frank."

"Shut the fuck up." He draws back at me.

Tears were flowing like waterfalls from my eyes.

He rips off my shirt and bra, and he pulls off my pants and panties. He pulls off his pants and boxers. "Open your legs."

I don't so he snatches them open, pins me down, and rams himself inside of me.

The pain was unbearable. It hurt felt like something was ripping inside of me. I could only scream out in pain. I have never felt anything like this in my life. Each stroke was harder and deeper than ever before. When he reaches his peak, he releases inside of me.

With a menacing look, he stood up and looks down on me before he leaves out of my room and out of the house. I run to the bathroom, blood running down my leg, and sit under the shower.

About fifteen minutes later Aaron and Mieko comes over. I guess they saw the stuffed knocked over in the living room and knew something had to be wrong.

"Applez," Aaron yelled out.

"Yolanda," Mieko followed.

They came running into the bedroom.

"Applez," Aaron says again.

They come into the bathroom, because they heard the shower running.

"What happened?"

"It was Frank. He beat me then raped me," I cried out.

"Aye yo dog, she bleeding. We need to get her to the hospital."

"Get a towel." Aaron instructs Mieko.

Mieko grabs a towel and put it around me and picks me up, and takes me to the car and rushes me to the hospital.

The last thing I can remember is getting to the hospital and them telling the nurse what was going on. After that I blacked out.

I wake up in a hospital bed with Jeremy holding my hand with his forehead to it. I squeezed his hand.

"Hey. You finally back."

"Yeah." I say in a weak voice.

They doctor said he would be back in to explain everything whenever you woke up." NaNa explained.

I shake my head yeah. "Where is Aaron and Mieko?"

"Them and Trill sitting in the hall."

"You'll go get them."

She gets up and goes to get them.

Aaron walks in first.

"Come here," I say.

He comes over and I give him and Mieko a hug.

"Thank you." I tell them.

"I would have been there earlier, but me and my girl was fussing about something. I should have been there earlier." Aaron says.

"It's not your fault."

"I promised your dad I'll look out for you. I can't see you like this." He walks back out the room.

"While I was blacked out, I went back to the time when I was at this family reunion when I was like eight or nine. Me and my cousins were climbing trees and I fell out and broke my leg. When I was in the hospital my dad was telling me how everything would be all right, and my mom was telling me how I would walk stronger from all of this. And those words just kept repeating. I really thought I was going to die that day." I laugh at my childish stupidity. "I know some good will come from this all."

Mieko walks back out to check on Aaron. He comes back and gets Trill and says they will be back.

Later on the doctor comes back in to check on me. He tells me everything they did to me and that I may need surgery to repair my cervix, but they have to see how it heals, but he scheduled an appointment with my gynecologist to make sure everything was ok. He tells me I will be released in the morning.

The next day Jeremy drives me back to my house, and I still hadn't heard from Aaron or the others. When I got inside I slowly sat down because I was sore from the encounter. It wasn't like the other times we did it, it was hella painful.

"Owe. It hurts every time I move."

"The doctor says it will ware away while you taking your pain medicine." NaNa explains to me like I wasn't there.

"It ain't working now."

"You need some help?" Jeremy offers to help

"I got it." I propped my legs up on the recliner.

"You need anything." NaNa asks me.

"I'm hungry."

"I'll order some pizza."

"Ok."

NaNa gets up and uses the house phone to order some pizza.

I ask Jeremy. "Are you going to stay here with me?"

"Yeah. I need to go get some clothes though."

I shake my head yeah.

"I'm going to go ahead and get them while NaNa is here with you."

"Ok."

He gives me a kiss on the cheek then get up and leave.

"I can't believe I started putting him over yall. I should of listened to you when you first told me about everything."

"Before yall started dating all you saw was the good in him. Believe me, I know what getting hit feels like. That's the only reason I was giving you advice. I figured something was up, but I didn't know how bad. Damien changed his lifestyle up ever since his mom died. He realized what he was doing was wrong. Everything he was doing he learned from his dad and he saw him beat on her when he was younger so he thought that was alright to do, but later on he learned that wasn't right. Don't get me wrong he ain't no saint and we all know that. But he did change up."

"Yeah."

Soon Jeremy comes back and the pizza man brings the food. We eat then I go to the room and lay down. Aaron comes over and tells me that they couldn't find Frank anywhere, but Mieko's cousin that knows one of Frank's partners said he was headed out on a flight back to New York.

In the next few days Jeremy gets his college situation straight and was going to start the next semester.

Chapter 20

A week and a half after the rape I finally go to see my OBGYN.

"So how have you been feeling Ms. Smith?" The doctor asks.

"The soreness has slowly been going away, but I've been feeling really nauseous and tired lately."

"Well, I'm going to run some test on you today to see how you're doing."

"Ok."

She does some test on me and ask a few questions.

"The reason for your fatigue feelings is because you are about three weeks pregnant."

I put my head on my knees. Out of everything that happened I never thought that pregnancy would come up. Oh my god. When I slept with Jeremy that night after he moved back we didn't use any protection.

"You do have a choice to abort this pregnancy."

"I don't know. A little while before the incident I had unprotected sex with someone. If it wasn't that type of situation, I probably would want an abortion, but I need time to think this through."

"You have the number to call me if you have any questions or anything. I'm not trying to rush you on your decision, but it will be much easier to terminate your pregnancy at an earlier stage."

"I know."

"Well, I'm through for today and your next appointment will be scheduled for next Thursday at eleven thirty."

"Ok. Thank you." I stand up and shake her hand then I leave out the building and go to my car and call Jeremy from there to meet me at my house since he was home from school.

When I get there he is already there.

"What's up?" He asked as I sat down beside him on the couch.

"Well, you know I been to the doctor today. She did blood work and everything. I was telling her how I was feeling fatigue and nauseous. I took a pregnancy test, and it came back that I am pregnant, and you know it's either a possibility for you or him to be the father. She asked me if I wanted an abortion, but I don't know. I said if it was just the Frank situation..."

"Either way I want you to have it. I'll help you take of it even if it's not mine."

I give Jeremy a hug because I knew he was a real standup guy.

"I checked your mail and your letter from college came." He hands it to me from off the end table.

I open it up and read it. "I got accepted." I hopped up out of the chair and Jeremy stands up and gives me a hug. "I got to let everybody know." I pick up my cell phone and call NaNa first.

NaNa answers the phone, "Hello."

"Guess what girl."

"What?"

"I got accepted into the college."

"I knew it girl. I knew you could do it," she says with excitement.

"I just opened it." I walk into the room. "And I just came back from the doctor."

"What did they say?"

"Well, they ran a few tests that will take a little bit for the results to get back, but she did tell me that I am about three weeks pregnant."

"Oh my God. Are you keeping it?"

"Yeah, because it's a possibility that Jeremy might be the father."

"What? You…without…Jey?"

"It happened a few days before what happened with Frank. It was the day that he came back, so there is no way to really know." I sit down on the bed.

"How he feel about this?"

"He is the one who wants me to keep it. He said either way he'll help me take care of it."

"Jey is a real stand up dude."

"Yeah. If it wasn't the fact that he was a possibility I probably would get an abortion."

"You are going to look so funny being pregnant."

"I know right. I already look about fifteen."

"Yeah."

We laugh.

Jeremy comes in the room and lay behind me. I put my hand over the phone.

"You tired?"

"Yeah. I'm tired of walking around all day, and worrying about you."

"Aw." I pinch his cheek and take my hand off the phone. "Yeah, well I'll call you back later."

"Ok."

I hang up with her.

"I hope the baby's mine, but it wouldn't matter either way."

"I hope so too. Seriously, out of everything that happened, even with me and you, I didn't think about getting pregnant. And it's not like I'm not ready to or don't want to, it's like me, Red, Applez, Yolanda Smith with a baby. That would be least likely expected. And then college and I'm going to be pregnant in my freshman year.

"It'll be straight though. You know mama will watch it while we in school."

"Well, we'll see how it turns out."

Jeremy phone rings and he checks the caller ID. "It's Bianca."

"Answer it."

He answers and put it on speaker. "Hello."

229

"Hey baby, this Bianca."

"Yeah."

"You know I been tripping for a while now, but I really didn't want you to go. The time that you have been gone, I've been thinking. The only reason I've been acting this way toward you is because I love you. I can't help the fact that I get jealous, but I promise to do my best and change for you."

"You trying to act like you didn't cuss me out when I came and got my shit."

"But I didn't mean it. I was just mad that you were actually leaving, but I didn't really want you to go. I miss you and I want you back."

I change my facial expression.

"I can't do that.

"I promise you I'll change. I love you."

"You done waited to long for that. I'm through with you and all the games you be running."

"But baby I love you and I want you back so bad."

"But you want get him back," I interrupt.

"Who is that?"

"You heard me. Jeremy has moved on and deserves someone who is going build him up and not bring him down, so please lose the number and keep it pushing." I press the end the call. "If she calls back, I'll answer it."

I lay down facing Jeremy.

"What?"

"Nothing, I just like looking at you, but for real, she bet not call back."

He laughs. "I got you. So, are you going to let the crew know?"

"Yeah, I'm going to call Aaron in a little bit."

"I know we ain't really been talking about how we feel about each other, so I want to know everything you feeling."

"Well, for a long time, I sort of had a crush on you, and this started way before prom, but you know how I felt that you acted childish about everything. So that part I really was feeling, but then again it was still that attraction there, but I moved it to the back of my mind and left it alone. Every time I saw you after the fact of how we said we would be better off friends, I was still had feelings for you.

After we got older and I watched you grow up, there was more of an attraction to you, but of course I was not ready to be in a relationship and by that time you and Bianca were together. You remember that night we went to the strip club and ole girl was dancing on you?"

"Yeah."

"I was so jealous. Oh my god. That's why I had to go get another drink."

He laughs.

"I'm not even going to lie, I have had a few dreams about you."

"Tell me." He smiles.

I shake my head no and he starts tickling me.

"Okay. Okay." I calm down. "So um, one time in one of my dreams..." I explain to him how everything went down.

"Damn." He laughs.

231

"Tell me how you feeling."

"I mean you know how I feel about you. I've always told you this. I've liked you since the first time I met you. You kind of broke my heart for real, because I wanted to be more than friends."

"I'm sorry."

"I thought you and me were going to be something after prom, but it didn't turn out that way. I couldn't get you off my mind."

"Well, you got me now." I move closer to him and kiss him.

"Yeah.

I put my hand on his face and run it down his cheek and over his lips, and he let my finger slip into his mouth. "They said I wouldn't be able to have sex for another week or so, but my body be telling me otherwise."

"It seem like every time I get around you I get into the mood. Sometimes I just have to get up and take a cold shower."

"Yeah I know. One time I purposely started moving around while you were behind me. You backed away a little, but I moved again. You was so rock hard."

"I figured you was doing it on purpose."

"Sometimes when I walk it still hurts a little bit anywayz, so I'm going to wait it out." I look up from him and sit up. "I'm about to call Aaron."

I call Aaron and it just rings and he doesn't answers so I call up Mieko.

"What up Applez?" Mieko answers the phone.

"Hey Miek. I was just calling to let you know some news.

"What's poppin?"

"First, I just got my letter back from the school...I got accepted," I say happily.

"That's what's up. You about to be running thangs huh?"

"Ya already kno." I laugh. "And I been to the doctor today and she ran some test on me and everything, and she told me that I am pregnant. It's a possibility that Jeremy is the dad too."

"Pregnant?" He said with amazement.

"Yeah. About three weeks."

"Wow. I'm happy for you and everything."

"Thanks."

"You called Aaron?"

"Yeah, but he didn't answer."

"I think his girlfriend over there."

"Oh. So what you up to? Chillin?"

"For right now I am. I'm about to go out with one of my lady friends."

"Oh ok. Whatever happened to them two girls?"

"That was just a few times thing."

"You are just a big ass freak, willing to try anything once."

"You remembered that DVD I let Aaron hold and we all watched it?"

"Yeah."

"Them two girls and that dude."

"Eww." I make an ugly face.

Yeah we was doing some shit like dat."

"You is so nasty, but you need to chill out on that for real."

"That's what I'm trying to do. I'm looking for someone now I can keep round for a while."

"I know you ain't trying to grow up on me?" I smile.

"That's why I'm taking this girl out. You know I usually don't do this, because I don't be wanting to spend my money on no female like that."

"Yeah, I'm proud of you Mieko."

"Yeah." His phone beeps. "That's her right there. I'll call you back later."

"Alright." I hang up the phone. "I'm hungry."

"Me too."

"I guess I'll go and cook some steak, mash potatoes and garden peas."

We go into the kitchen and Jeremy helps me cook dinner. We talked and reminisced on high school, and everything we've done.

"I'm about to go ahead and take a shower, and get ready to go to bed."

"Ok."

He leaves out and goes into the bathroom. I go into the room and lay down. Even though I wasn't sleep for about thirty minutes, I had a dream about my future. It was best dream I've had lately, since I've just recently started getting over my nightmares.

When Jeremy gets out the shower, he wakes me up. "Get right baby."

I yarn and move over to my side of the bed. "It feel like I was sleep for a long time."

When he gets in bed I lay my head on his chest.

"You know what?"

"What?"

"I love you."

"I love you too."

"I love the things you do for me, the way you care. How you know the right things to say to make me feel better. I love everything about you."

"Those are the things I'm supposed to do. Take care of my girl."

I give him a kiss on the lips and we go to sleep.

When I wake up Jeremy had already gone to school. I get up, take a shower, brush my teeth and get dressed. I called Aaron and let him know everything. He congratulates me on my pregnancy and me getting into school. Things were seeming to be going pretty good.

Chapter 21

Two weeks later, I go back for my appointment with my gynecologist. Jeremy stayed from school to go with me.

"Hey Dr. Anderson."

"Hello Ms. Smith."

We take a seat.

I introduce Jeremy. "This is my boyfriend Jeremy."

"Hey, how are you doing?" She shakes his hand.

"I'm doing good."

"How are you feeling today?" She asks me.

"I'm alright. Just that sometimes I get a little light-headed."

"Most of everything with your test came back very good."

"Ok." I shake my head.

"I have a few concerns about you pregnancy though."

I shake my head yeah, but very much concerned.

"With the surgery you have gone through recently, there is a chance that when you deliver your baby, you could severely hemorrhage and lose a lot of blood. During your pregnancy, the bigger your baby gets can put pressure on the scar."

"So what are you saying?"

"There's a possible chance that either you or your baby can lose your life. We need to know if you still want to continue this pregnancy."

A tear rolls down my face and I stand up and leave out of her office. Jeremy follows behind me. I sit in a chair outside of her office with my head on my lab and cry.

"Why shit like this always got to happen to me?"

Jeremy puts his arms around me. "I'm here for you no matter what. I'm feeling the same way as you, and if I lose either one of you I don't know what I'll do." He begins to cry.

I sit up and put my arms around him and kiss him. "I promise I'm going to be here for you, I know we are going to make it through."

We get ourselves together and go back in the doctor's office.

"Dr. Anderson...I want to keep my baby."

237

We sit down and talk everything out. She gives us all the information we need to know to make this be a positive outcome.

When we get back to the house after talking with the crew, I lay down and rest and me and Jeremy talk about everything the doctor told us about at the hospital.

"Jey. If anything does happen to me, I want you to take good care of our baby."

"You know I will baby, but I don't want to even think like that. My mama said she wanted to come over to see us."

"I haven't seen Mrs. Francine in a long while."

"She always used to ask about you. That's probably because I use to talk about you all the time."

"What she said when you told her you were going to be a dad?"

"You know how she a cool person, and then she likes you, so she really was happy. She just was talking about all the responsibility I was going to have to take on to be a good dad. I kept telling her I could handle this." He laughs.

"Is she coming tomorrow?"

"Yeah, she knows this side of town good, so she'll know how to get here."

I lay on his chest and drift off to sleep.

At about five thirty the next morning, I wake up and run to the bathroom to throw up.

"Shit," I say after spitting.

Jeremy comes in where I'm at.

"You ok baby."

"Yeah." I gasp for air. "Yeah."

"You scared me."

"Sorry." I wiped my mouth. "I hate throwing up."

I brush my teeth. "I look so fucked up."

"You look good to me."

"I mind as well take a shower now."

I go get some clothes to put on after I take my shower. I go back and get in bed.

"I didn't mean to wake you up. I have never had to wake up out of my sleep to throw up."

"But you are better now?"

"Yeah baby."

I rub my stomach and he does it for me.

"Showing already." He tries to be funny.

I hit him. "Shut up. No I'm not. You trying to be funny ain't you? And shouldn't you be going back to sleep since you got to go to school at nine."

"Yeah." He pulls my arm. "Baby you mad at me." He smiles.

"Yeah."

"Aw. I was just playing. You know I love you."

"I love you too."

I lean into him and give him a kiss.

"I've been thinking. I know what I want to name the baby."

"Yeah?"

"Jaden if it's a boy and Andrea if it's a girl. Jaden Zy'mier."

"Jaden Zy'mier Roberts just like his mom and dad."

"What?"

"I was also thinking and I want the woman carrying my baby to have my last name."

I sit up. "So, you saying what I think you are trying to say?"

"Yeah, I know I don't have a ring for you right now, but I want you to be my wife."

"But..."

He cuts me off. "That doesn't matter, either way I want you to be mine always and forever, so what do you say?"

"Yes baby. I want to be our wife." I lean to the side and we kiss.

After Jeremy comes home from school his mom comes over and he cooks for us and we have a nice talk about everything that has happened to me. She tells me that she would be there throughout my hold pregnancy.

We break the news about the engagement to our friends and they were happy for us and wished us the best.

Chapter 22

Five months had gone by and I was starting to show a little bit.

"Look at your little stomach. Think in about four months, you'll have a little boy running round, and I'll be an Auntie." NaNa says happily

"Yeah, I get tired sometimes and have to sit down.

"You better hope he don't act like Jeremy used to, back when we was in school."

"If he does, I'm sending him to you." I laugh.

"Send him on. You got me wanting to have one."

"Don't let me influence you."

"How your hubby doing?"

Jeremy and e brought me this beautiful engagement ring and after I had Jaden, we planned to have the wedding of my dreams.

"He's doing good. All he be up to is school and work."

"That boy be working so hard."

"Yeah he do." I drink some of my bottled water.

"I know he going to look like Jey."

"You should see how he playing with my stomach and everything. He'll go to sleep on my chest rubbing my stomach looking so cute."

"Aw."

"When my stomach gets a little bigger, we supposed to go take some pregnancy pictures."

"Those are going to be too cute."

"Yeah, I can't believe Mieko and his girl still together."

"I know right. He would be the one I would think have babies scattered everywhere."

"Well, I know he know how to stay strapped up."

"Yeah. Aaron surprised me to."

"Uhn huh. They found out when Fallon was going on her third month that she was pregnant."

"He is so happy too. Ain't she dude in two months."

"Yeah. He is going to make a great daddy."

"Yep. When Mrs. Francine coming over."

"She said she'll be here after while. She's been helping me big time since I been pregnant. Whatever I need, she's there."

My phone rings and it's Jeremy.

"Hey baby." I answer.

"What you doing?"

"Nothing. NaNa sitting over here with me."

"You doing ok?"

"Yeaaah baby."

"Alright, I was just checking in on you."

"I know. I told you I'm good."

"I'm just making sure. Ma made it ova there?"

"No. She said she would be here after while. You on your way home?"

"Yeah. I'll be home in a minute."

"Alright, drive safe."

"Love you baby."

"Love you too.

I hang up the phone.

"Checking up on his baby."

"Yeah."

"Yall is so cute together. This should of happened a long time ago."

I smile.

My doorbell rings and I go answer it, and it's Jeremy's mom.

"Hey Ms Fran." I give her a hug since I haven't seen her in a week.

"How you doing baby?"

"I'm good."

"Jey done made it home yet?"

"No ma'am. I just got off the phone with him, and he just got out of school."

"Ok."

We walk into the living room.

"Hey Ms. Fran."

"Hey Natosha. How have you been doing?"

"I'm doing fine."

"That's good."

We sit down.

"What yall been up to today?"

"Just sitting around talking."

"Yall done ate."

"Yes ma'am. But I'm still hungry. I was just about to go fix something."

"I'll do it for you. You just go ahead and rest."

"I got it Ma." I stand up.

"How about I help you then?"

"Alright." I put my hand on my hip.

"I'm about to go ahead and go girl." NaNa stands up.

"Ok."

NaNa leaves and me and Ms. Fran go in the kitchen to cook. We decided to cook some pork chops, rice and peas. When we're half way done Jeremy comes home.

"Hey baby. Hey Ma." He gives us hugs. "It smells good in here."

"Thank you." I give him a kiss on the cheek.

"How long you been her Ma?"

"Since we started cooking."

"Jey, do you mind doing something for me?"

"No. What is it?"

"I've been craving pineapple juice, the kind straight out the can with the pineapples in it."

"I'll go get it."

"I want the Dole kind nothing else."

"You can go with him, I'll finish up."

"Ok. I'll go get my purse." I go to the room to get my purse. I go in the living room where Jeremy was waiting.

"You ready?"

"Yeah."

We leave and go to the grocery store.

"I need to get some off that coco butter for stretch marks, because I do not want none."

"You ain't got none though."

"You must be haven't looked right here real good." I point to my side where they are at. "And now that my titties getting bigger, I got some little ones there."

"It don't bother me, especially now, because you got them knockers."

"Shut up." I push him.

"That ass getting juicer too. It already was phat from the beginning." He hits me on the butt.

"Stop." I grab his hand. "Will you get me two of those right there?"

He gets the two jars, and then we go to find the coco butter, pay for everything and leave.

When we get back to the house we eat and sit down and talk with his mom and she leaves.

"How was school?" I rub my hand across his hair.

"It was straight. I got a big presentation due sometime next week."

"What kind?"

"PowerPoint. We got to come up with our own company and we got to be able to market and sale our product. We got to come up with prices and everything."

"How many people in your class?"

"Like twenty-two or twenty- three. We could of worked with partners, but I wanted to work alone."

"Yeah. Plus you ain't got to worry about anyone not doing their part."

"I'm going to start on it tomorrow, so I can have everything done early."

"My feet are hurting."

"Because you always on them. You don't ever rest."

"I'm about to go get in the tub."

"Alright."

I get up and go run the water in my Jacuzzi tub and add some Victoria's Secret bubble bath. When it feels up I get undressed and get in. I close my eyes and relax. I hear the bathroom door open and I open my eyes. Jeremy is standing there naked.

"What are you doing?" I laugh.

"I'm about to get in with you." He gets in and gets close on me. "You're even fine pregnant."

"More like sexy." I flick my hair ova my shoulder.

"Yeah." He puts his hand on my thigh.

I grab his face and kiss him.

"I'm ready to experience fatherhood."

"I know you'll be a great father. I can't wait to become a mother either.

Two and a half months go by and pregnancy was really weighing heavily on me. I had to take my time and rest more, because I would become tired easily. The doctor ended up putting me on bed rest and Jeremy made sure to be strict about that.

I blow out air. "Baby, I done got huge." I say looking into the full length mirror in the bathroom. I was going on seven and a half months.

"Yeah I know," he says it as joke and begins to laugh.

I hit. "Shut up. You ain't funny. I ain't ask for your input. He is putting a lot of pressure on me now. Getting heavier each day."

He comes and stands behind me. "And still looking good." He kisses me on the cheek from behind.

"I am hungry."

"You just ate like an hour ago."

"Jaden must have eaten an hour ago, because Yolanda is the one hungry right now." I laugh.

"You crazy."

We leave from out of there and I go reheat some spaghetti that I cooked the day before. I get the ranch and some bread.

"You put ranch on everything."

"It tastes better like this. This is one thing that bastard did was teach me how to cook a little." I sit down. "I'm glad you out for the summer."

"Me too, because I get to be home with you more."

I start eating.

He picks up my feet and start massaging them. "They are swollen."

"Because you always on them and won't rest."

He puts pressure on the middle of my foot.

"Damn that feels good. Do you have to work tonight?"

"Yeah at seven."

"Oh." I get louder. "Aaah."

"What?"

"Pain."

"Where at?"

I point to my stomach. "Right here. Shit." I stand up. "I'm about to go to the bathroom real quick."

"Ok."

I go to the bathroom to use it and I was bleeding. I flush the toilet and call for Jeremy.

I yell. "Jey!"

He comes running. "What?"

"I'm bleeding, and I need to get to the hospital."

"Damn." He hits the wall.

"Ow it hurts," I scream out.

"Come on let's go."

We rush to the hospital. When I get there they rush me to the back. They tell me that they were going to have to take my baby and give me an emergency caesarian, because I was losing too much blood. They had to stop the bleeding and be careful during the C-section, because the odds we were looking at in the beginning of the pregnancy were what we were facing at that moment. Being that I was only seven months and three weeks Jaden would be premature.

After they delivered Jaden, they didn't let me see him, and quickly rushed him away. They finally got the bleeding to stop and then I was put into ICU, so I could be closely monitored.

Jeremy stayed with me the whole time I was there. NaNa, Mieko, Aaron, and Trill came to see me while I was in surgery. They came to the back to see me after they allowed people to come back.

I had to stay in the hospital for the next week and Jeremy and Ma Fran would rotate out since Jeremy had to go back to work. I had to make him go home on the days that he were off so that he could get some good rest, but he would be back or call every hour.

Three days had gone by and I still haven't seen my baby yet, and today I was going to get to see him. Jeremy was with me and the nurse took me over in the wheelchair.

When I saw Jaden it made me and Jeremy cry. He was hooked up to all types of machines.

"He's so little." I say.

"Like we were telling you. His lungs aren't quite developed, so we are giving him medicine for that and he is still getting fed through a tube."

"Can we touch him?" Jeremy asks.

"Yes of course."

Jeremy reached through the incubator and touched Jaden's hand and he grabs his finger and starts kicking his little legs.

I wiped my tears away as I smiled.

The nurse says, "He looks like the both of yall."

"His eyes are so pretty and grey. Head full of hair." I say

I touch his feet and rub my finger cross his cheek.

"I can't wait till he gets better and gets to come home." Jeremy says.

"Me too. Did you bring the camera with you?"

"Yeah." He gets it out and record Jaden and me, then I get it and record them and the nurse.

We stay with Jaden until time for me to check out. We planned on coming back after I got some rest, because I couldn't sleep good in the hospital. When it's time to go they wheel me out to the car and I go home.

Everybody comes to check on me. They stay for a long time, but then I get sleepy and go to the room. Aaron said he was going when we go back to see Jaden.

"You need something right now?" Jeremy asks.

"Some water."

"Ok." He leaves out to get the water.

I put some extra pillows underneath me to sit up a little. Soon Jeremy comes back, but by then, I was fast asleep. I slept up until the time to go back to the hospital. I was awakened by a kiss on the cheek.

I yarn. "What time is it?"

"4:30."

"It felt I was sleep for days."

"I had went to get your water, and when I got back you was sleep. Snoring and all.

"I was?"

"Yes."

"I only snore when I'm dead ass tired." I wipe my nose. "I need to go ahead and call Aaron and tell him to come over." I sit up. "Shit that hurts." I frown.

Jeremy helps me up and I get my phone and call Aaron and he is over in ten minutes to take us to the hospital and we go see Jaden.

"Hey baby." I say while waving at Jaden.

"I can tell lil' shawty going to be pulling all the little girls," Aaron says.

Jeremy asks the nurse, "Has he been doing the same?"

"Slowly progressing. It's a miracle really, because most babies born this early are least likely to make it, but Jaden is a true miracle. It shouldn't be two long before he gets to come home. Maybe three to five weeks depending on his progress."

I smile. "I can't wait to take him home. But I'm going to be here every day until he gets to come home."

"Me too."

"So who is this?" The nurse was talking about Aaron.

"My best friend who is like a brother and Jaden's god dad slash Uncle

"Aaron."

"Nurse Stacy Hills. But since yall are going to be frequent visitors, yall can call me Stacy."

I touch Jaden's hand and rub my finger across his jet black hair, which he gets from Jeremy.

"Ok," Jeremy responds.

Ma Fran walks in the room. "Hey. I came to see me Grandbaby."

Jeremy whispers in my ear, "We don't need a blood test, because I can tell he's mine." He gives me a kiss on the neck.

Day by day Jaden got better and he started gaining weight and he feeding from a bottle instead of the tubes. In three weeks he was able to come home with me and Jeremy. We were so excited for him to be home. Jeremy had decorated the extra room for his arrival.

Two weeks after Jaden was born, Fallon gave birth to Aaron's son. He was happy to be a dad and I had become a mother and a Auntie in a short amount of time.

Everybody would come over to see the baby, but I hogged them from holding him too long, because I was glad to have my baby home with me.

For the first few weeks, Jaden slept in his basinet in our room. A couple of months went by and he was doing just fine and he was just as healthy as if was born full term.

I came home one day to Jeremy asleep in the recliner with Jaden sleeping on his bare chest.

"Aw, look at my two babies." I go over and take Jaden from Jeremy and put him in his crib in his room. When I came back into the living room Jeremy was waking up.

"Where's Jaden?" He yarns.

"I laid him down in his crib. Yall was looking so cute sleep. I should have took a picture."

"So how has your little bit of freedom been?"

"It's been good, but I miss my two men." I sit in his lap

"You did huh."

"Yeah." I kiss him

"Don't start nothing you can't finish."

"Who said I was starting something?" I kiss him again.

"The way you got me on rock right now."

I pull at his basketball shorts to see. "Mm, I can't help that I just got that effect on you."

He started kissing on me and licking on my neck, because he knew that was my spot. "Let's go to the room."

We get up and go to the room. I start taking off my clothes on the way to the bedroom and when we get in there Jeremy pulls off my panties. Jeremy drops his shorts and boxers to the floor and he lies down on the bed and I straddled him.

It started getting so hot and then we started to hear Jaden's cries coming from the bay monitor.

"You want me to go get him."

"I'll get him." I put on my panties and one of Jeremy's T-shirts and goes see what was wrong with Jaden. He was crying because he needed to be changed. After I changed him, I went and made him a bottle then came back to the room. Jeremy had put back on his clothes.

"What was wrong?"

"He was wet and you already know it's about feeding time. He must of knew mama was about to get some."

"He must of knew I was about to try and make him another sibling."

"Don't tell that lie. It will be a while before I think about having another child."

He laughs. "You not going to give me a little girl?"

"Not now, you are asking for too much, but you will have another one, one of these days."

"I was just kidding baby. He'll get a little brother or sister sooner or later."

"Later." I laugh. "That's why I'm about to get this Nuva Ring so you won't knock me up anytime soon."

"That's gonna be perfect for me. Now I can bust freely." Jeremy laughs.

"Nasty self. I hope Jaden don't pick up your manish ways."

"But you love it though." He kisses me.

Chapter 23

Time seemed to fly, because mine and Jeremy's wedding was right around the corner. We had planned for a springtime wedding and the colors were purple and grey.

I had run my wedding planner crazy trying to make my wedding perfect, because I wanted it to go by flawlessly. I had the perfect wedding dress that I always dreamed of and the perfect husband that I would meet at the end of the isle.

On the day of our wedding I was so nervous. It didn't hit me that it was real until that morning that Jeremy and I would be one, and would be husband and wife. We would be officially a complete family with Jaden.

I had my head down on the vanity.

"What's wrong girl?" NaNa put her hand on my shoulder.

"I am so nervous. Look." I held my hand out to show that my hands were shaking. "My hands are shaking."

"I don't see why you are. It's like you and him are already married."

"All these people though."

"Are friends and family."

"I never thought this day would make me feel like this." My eyes started wailing up with tears.

"Aww, it's going to be ok girl." She gives me a hug. "Yall have known each other for the majority of your life. Yall have a child together. You've been through good and bad with him. You should be happy right now. That man truly loves you. Besides, you don't need to be messing up your makeup with all that crying."

We both laugh.

"You always know how to make me laugh."

"Hey, that's what I'm here for."

I smile. "Thank you NaNa." I stand up and give her a hug.

"Now come on and get ready, so we won't be late Cinderella."

I got dressed into my Vera Wang dress and we traveled to meet with the man who would be taking us to the venue. We would be indeed pulling up fairy tale style in a horse and carriage just like Cinderella.

When we came to the venue, everyone was in place. The wedding director followed us and called ahead to let them know to let the bridesmaids and groomsmen walk down the aisle.

Before we made it around the corner, I had Miami's little boy to ring the bell and run down the aisle saying, "The bride is coming, the bride is coming."

We rode up to the entrance way of the aisle where Aaron met us. He was walking me down the aisle in my father's place. The driver got out and he and Aaron helped me down the stairs of the carriage.

"I'm so nervous Aaron." I say to him.

"It's going to be ok lil sis. You look beautiful."

He gives me a hug.

Dre' Soulmate started playing, and that was my cue to walk down the aisle. As we walked I looked around and everything turned out to be so beautiful. I wished that my mom and dad was there to see their baby get married, but I know they were watching from heaven with a smile on their faces.

When we got to the end, I noticed how good Jeremy looked and I couldn't stop smiling.

The minister begins reciting wedding vows. "Dearly beloved, we are gathered here today, to join these two young souls in holy matrimony. Who gives this young lady away?"

Aaron steps up and says, "I do," then joins the groomsmen.

The minister continues, but when it was time, Jeremy and I prepared our own vows.

Jeremy begins, "I'm kind of nervous, so I might stumble over the words a little bit."

People were saying things like, 'That's ok baby.' 'Go ahead.'

"Since the first time that I met you in junior high, I knew that I needed you in my life. You may not have thought the same at the time, but you eventually came around." He chuckles.

Everyone laughs.

"I promised myself that day, that I would get the girl of my dreams, and now I final have her. I will love you forever and always." He starts tearing up.

"It's alright baby." I wipe the tears from his eyes.

"All I'm trying to say is, this bond that we have is unbreakable. I love you with all my heart and soul. We've been through a lot together in a short time, but we can make it, have, and will. I love you so, so much and I'm glad that you are willing to give me the opportunity to be everything that you need in a man. I love you Yolanda."

"I love you too." I say back to him.

Someone hands him a tissue and I get one.

"He is about to make me cry all over again." I giggle. "I never thought I would ever find true love, after the things that happened in my life, but all things changed when I paid attention, and let someone love me for me. In the past, I was busy putting what was real to the side, so I'm glad that you gave me another go around. Jeremy I am grateful for everything that you've done for me. You've been there through some of the roughest times of my life. I truly love you. Words can't even express enough the love that I have for you. In the time that we've been together, we made our handsome son Jaden Zy'mier Roberts, and I'm so glad for you and him. You are a great friend, father, boyfriend, so I know that you will be the best husband. I love you bae."

"I love you too."

The preacher continues and we say our 'I do's'. "With the power invested in me, I now pronounce you two man and wife. You may now salute your bride."

Jeremy and I share a very passionate kiss and everybody went wild with cheering.

We jumped over the broom, then walked down the aisle together and got in to carriage and rode over to the hall where the reception would be taken place. When we got there I changed into a dress that I could be a little more comfortable in.

The reception was going great.

"I'm about to go out to the car and get Jaden's diaper bag."

"Ms. Fran I'll get it. I need to get my purse from your car anyway."

"Baby you enjoy your wedding I'll go get it."

"I got it." I get up. "I'll be right back baby." I kissed Jeremy on the cheek.

I go out to Ms. Fran's car to get Jaden's diapers. As I was getting them out of the backseat, I head someone call my name.

"Yolanda." The sound of the voice sent a chill up my spine and fear all over my body. I turned around and there stood Frank.

"You ain't gonna say hey." He says.

I say nothing.

"That's okay. That must be for Jaden." He points to the baby bag I had in my hand.

"How do you know my son's name?"

"I have my sources." He walks towards me, but I back away with every step that he made towards me. "I know everything that you do. I know the day that you had him, and the day that you were able to bring him home. I even went to see him when he was first born to see if he was mine, but you could look at him and tell that he belonged to that bitch you just married." He comes closer to me.

"Why don't you just go? Please leave us alone Frank. Let me live my life. I'm happy now, and I don't need any drama in it."

He shakes his head. "Ok." He pulls out a gun and aims it at me.

My heart start racing, but it seemed like everything had started to move in slow motion. When he cocked the gun, I dropped Jaden's baby bag and ran for my life.

Boom, boom, boom... The sounds of his gun ranged out, and then I blacked out.

"Hey baby girl."

"Daddy?" My vision was blurry and I couldn't make out the person in front of me, but I definitely recognized the voice.

"That's right baby girl. Come and give me a hug." I walk over to him to give him a hug and he became clearer to me.

"Hey Yolanda. Mama's favorite girl."

"Mama, you look so beautiful." I told her as I placed my hands to her face.

"Hey Applez." It was Ace my ex.

I backed up. "Wait, wait a minute. What's going on? I mean...but you are all..."

"You are in heaven baby." My mama says to me.

"No, no I can't be. This has to be a dream. I just got married today. My baby, my husband, my friends...I can't be dead."

My dad says. "You were shot baby. You're fighting for your life, but things don't look too good."

"I can't die. I have a family that I have to be there for."

"If you want to still be around for that, you gave to fight harder baby girl."

"I know how much you miss us, but you have to stick around to finish out your life, and accomplish everything you have dreamed. You have a lot of things ahead of you." Ace says walking up to me.

I could hear Jaden crying and I could hear Jeremy talking to me. "Please don't leave me baby. I need you. Jaden needs you. Baby, I love you. Please don't go."

"If you want to stay you can, but if you want to go back, you have to fight harder for it." My mom says.

They all start to fade away, and I start running after them, all of a sudden I feel a pain in my side and my back that brings me to my knees.

"She is stabling out." The doctor says.

I start couching, trying to regain my breath back, because it felt like I was choking. I slowly open my eyes and look around the room.

"I'm right here baby." Jeremy says holding my hand tight.

261

"What happened?"

"When Frank shot you passed out."

The doctor says. "During surgery while trying to remove two of the bullets that remained in you, your body started going into shock and we thought we were going to lose you. Luckily the bullets missed your organs."

Jeremy continues. "When Aaron was going out to his car, he saw you talking to somebody, but couldn't make out who it was. When he was coming back in he heard the gunshots and saw you fall to the ground. He went to you and Mieko, Trill and Damien went after Frank."

"Where are they now?"

"Aaron is out in the hall. The police have Mieko, Trill and Damien in custody."

"So, they killed him?"

"One of them."

I closed my eyes and a tear rolled from them. "Where is my baby?"

"Mama is out in the hallway with him."

Right then Aaron rushed into the room. He comes over to me and give me a hug. "You ok Applez?"

"Yeah, the doctor just told me when they were trying to remove the bullets my body went in to shock and they couldn't find a pulse for a while. I'm ok now. I was just worried about you. What happened with the police?"

Aaron explained to me after hearing the gunshots he ran over to me and saw Frank walking away like nothing happened. That's when Mieko, Trill and Damien came out and he told them which way he went. "Mieko says after they ran their information, Trill confessed to being the one who shot him and Damien had a warrant out for a missed court date.

"Where is Mieko now?"

"He is in the waiting room. He didn't want to see you like this."

"I want to see Jaden and tell Mieko to come in too."

Jeremy gets up and gets his mama and Mieko comes in but stays near the door.

"You ok baby?" Ms. Fran asks me.

"As ok as I can be." I hold Jaden's hand.

"I'm getting ready to take him home, so he can get him some sleep."

"Ok. Bring him here so I can give him a kiss." I give him a kiss. "Mama loves you baby. I'll be home soon."

"I'll be back first thing in the morning with him. I'll see yall later." She leaves out of the room.

I look over to Mieko "Why you standing over there?"

He shakes his head and I see a tear roll down his eye.

"Come here Mieko." He comes to my bed side and I pull him to me by his shirt and give him a hug. "Thank you." I wipe a tear that was falling from his face.

After they released me from the hospital, I went to visited both Damien and Trill and thanked them for helping me.

"All rise." Everyone in the courtroom stood. "Judge Adrienne Allen presiding."

The judge says, "You may be seated," and everyone takes their seats.

"We are here today about the late Mr. Frank Johnson and Mrs. Yolanda Smith-Roberts and the events occurring prior to his murder and leading up to it. Mrs. Roberts can you take the Stand."

I come up and sit next to the judge after I'm sworn in by the bailiff to tell the truth about my testimony.

"Mrs. Roberts, can you tell us how you knew Mr. Frank Johnson."

"I met Frank at a club I use to go to and we became associates, then we later dated. He made advances towards me and wanted to get to know me outside of the club scene. At first I wasn't interested, because of our age difference, but I gave it a shot after a while."

The judge asks, "Can you tell us what you know about his drug life?"

"I can't speak on anything that I don't know about specifically." I actually knew a lot, but I wouldn't speak on it. I could remember my dad saying a code of the hustlers was 'Death Before Dishonor', so with what little respect that I had left for Frank, I was going to honor that code.

"Well tell us what you know."

"On our first official date we were talking getting to know each other and I told him that I wanted to know everything now then to find out later when it will hurt me in the long run and that's when he told me what he did, but I was never around any of it knowingly. He kept that life away from me."

"So why after knowing that why did you remain involved with him and engage in a relationship."

"I really liked Frank and eventually fell in love with him. He convinced me that nothing would happen to me, and he was wrong." My eyes began to water and was passed a tissue.

"Frank used to beat me. The first time that he hit me and left a visible mark was when I first caught him cheating on me." I look to my friends. "I told yall when me and the girl was fighting that she bust my lip and black my eye, but it wasn't her, it was Frank. I was hitting him and he back handed me to get me off of him." I shake my head.

"I'm so ashamed that I let it go on for so long. After I broke up with him, he fought me, but I got away by running to the bathroom and jumping out of the window. Then the rape happened, and then he showed up at my reception after my wedding."

"What did he say to you when you saw him that day."

"When I was getting my little boys baby bag out of the car, I heard him call my name. I turned around and there he stood. I was so scared. He asked was the bag for Jaden, calling him by name. He told me he knew everything. He said he knew the day that I had him and that he visited him in the hospital, and knew the day that I was able to bring him home.

I told him to leave and he acted like he was about to and that's when he pulls out his gun and points it at me. I couldn't move, but when he cocked the gun, I dropped the bag and ran. I heard each bullet leave the chamber and I passed out. All I know after that is that I woke up in the hospital."

The courtroom was silent, then the judge finally spoke. "How do you know Mr. Damien Mathews and Mr. Marcus Wright?"

"Both of them are friends of mine that I grew up with."

The judge gives me permission to leave the stand and he talks with both Damien and Trill, and calls Franks mom to the stand.

"Please state your name."

"Danielle Marie Howard." She was clearly emotional.

"Do you wear to tell the truth and nothing but the truth so help you god?

"I do."

"You may be seated."

She sits down.

"Ms. Howard, did you know of your son's abusive ways?" The judge asks.

"No ma'am I did not. When they came to the hospital when I was in there after I had a heart attack I knew something was going on, but I didn't think it was physical abuse."

"Did you know that your son sold drugs?"

"Yes."

"Is there anything that you would like to tell Mrs. Roberts?"

"I do." She wipes away tears. "I am sorry for what my son put you through. I am truly sorry. I went through some of the same things that you have with his father. I didn't think that Frank would take all of his ways after his dad. If it was up to me, I wouldn't want any of your friends to have to sit behind bars for trying to protect you from my son. I'm not saying killing him was the right thing to do, but it was out of self-defense, if you understand me.

"You may step down Ms. Howard."

Frank's mom went back to her seat.

We take a small recess and the judge comes back in and delivers her verdict. All pending chargers were dropped, but since Damien had a warrant against him, they only gave him community service, and they both would be released.

The courtroom rose as the judge left for her chambers. Frank's mom came over to me.

"I am sorry for all the hurt my son has caused to you. I really didn't know he was like that."

"It's not your fault and I'm sorry for the loss of your son. I would have come to the funeral to at least show my respect, but I didn't think it would be right."

"I understand. I will miss my son dearly, but I'm at peace and can't hold a grudge for what happened." She touches my shoulder and walks away.

I watch as she walks out of the courtroom.

Jeremy walks over to me. "You ok baby?"

"Yeah I'm fine. I'm just glad everything is over." I smile.

He wrapped his arms around me and I lay my head on his shoulders. NaNa walks over to me.

"I'm about to go wait for Damien to get released. I'll see you later."

"Girl, you know I will not see you later today. Your man been gone for almost a month, I know yall are going to be doing some catching up."

"You already know." She smiles and go wait for Damien.

We left out of the courtroom and waited outside for them to release Trill. Soon he comes out with Mieko and Aaron. I go over to him and give him a hug squeezing him tight.

"Damn girl, loosen up. You chocking the shit out of me."

I laugh. "I'm just glad that you are out. I was feeling guilty that you and Damien were in there for my problems."

"I told you that shit cool. We been down for a long time, so you know I got your back."

"The stuff you told us in there, you could of cane to us with it. You said you were ashamed of the things you let him do to you." Mieko says.

"I know, but then I was confused. I thought he would change, but he remained the same and seemed to get worst in the process. But now I'm putting all of this behind me. I have my husband, Jaden, my friends, and family. I'll be back in school next semester. Only place I can go from here is to the top and I'm not letting anything stop me. I'm taking control."

Next up from Sierra Denise...

Broken

The Story of Brooklyn

Broken: The Story of Brooklyn

I lay there on the ground surrounded by a pool of my own blood, praying that my life doesn't end like this. Crossing The Don was something I knew not to do, but I needed a way to get out, and when Layla came up with the plan, never did it cross our mind that we would get caught. Now I was the one paying for the flaws of our scheme.

"Bitch, I told you not to fuck with me or my money." The Don stood over me with his gun pointed down at my head.

"Please, please," I begged for dear life with what I had left in me. "Don't do this. I gave you all I had."

Heartless is what someone like him was, and I just knew my pleas to spare my life wouldn't reach him. He didn't pay any expense in taking anyone's life.

The Don spent many years running these streets by selling drugs and pimping out women, and I happened to be one of his main hoes, but now I was looking for a way out. It didn't all start off like that, I was The Don's Queen, his leading lady until I got mixed up into doing something that hurt him. In results of my fuck up, he put me in the streets to pay him back. He didn't care, It was like a marriage, till death do us part, and this maybe my time to go.

"Brook." I heard my name called out from a distance. It was my friend Layla.

The Don turns his head in that direction, then he turns back to me and I close my eyes as he pulls the trigger.

Chapter 1

It was hard growing up in such a bad environment. Family issues, personal issues. It was just tough dealing with it all. From being a kid I had to witness the fights between my parents. Hearing them argue about everything. My mother loved my dad with everything in her, but he didn't appreciate it.

'Well, why don't you keep your ass home sometimes?' I would hear my mom yell at my dad as I sat in the hallway listening to their fussing. As she continued arguing, he would storm out of their room and out the front door.

My dad was cheating on my mom and was rumored to have another woman pregnant with his baby. Even with all of this my mom was fighting to get her husband back full-time, but it wasn't working. My dad didn't care, he just moved on without a care for the family that he already had established with my mom.

I could hear my mom crying, so I walked into her room and let her cry on my shoulder. I was used to it now, and it didn't affect me as much as it did before. I would tell her that she deserved better and didn't have to be with him, because of me, my brother and sister. I wanted to see my mom happy and her letting my dad treat her this way was only making her a weaker person.

That day was the last that I saw my dad. He had walked out for good that time and that brought on a whole new depression for my mom. Other than going to work, she stayed in her room most of the time, so I had to take on more responsibilities around the house.

I had to take care of my brother Sydney who was a year younger than me and my sister London who was three years younger than him. I had to make sure they got the things they needed too. I cooked for them and cleaned up after them. I took on all the duties pertaining to the family that my mom neglected while she went through one of the most depressing moments of her life.

It was rough seeing my mother unhappy and knowing that it was my father that was causing her to feel this way. Late at night I could hear my mother crying and praying to God to send her husband back. *'God, I know Julian isn't a perfect man, but I'm willing to work on him. I promised to death do us part and I'm not going to give up on him. Please just bring him back to me and our family. I need him. We need him.'*

Sometimes I would also cry at night from all the pressure that was put on me to take on the responsibilities of the house as a young child, but I knew it was something I had to do. I made sure everything was good.

Although I was going through a lot at home, I never let it show in school. There, I was a totally different person from my home life. I was happy, bubbly, and everyone liked me. I carried myself like I was more mature than my age.

One day after school I had to walk home by myself instead of walking with my best friend, at the time, Lydia. She had to go to her grandparent's house that day, so she would be getting picked up. I didn't like walking alone, because there were these three older boys that would sit on the stoop of an abandon house and I didn't like the way they would watch me, but I had no choice this time, because that was the easiest way to get home.

"You'll be ok Brook. Just don't say anything and don't pay them any attention." Lydia says to me.

"Ok. See you Monday." I watched as Lydia got into the car with her grandmother and I proceeded to walk down the street, and across the road down the alley to get across to my house.

I looked and I saw Jarell sitting on the stairs of the building as he always did. I didn't see his friends with him. Without the other two, I felt a little safer walking through by myself, but that wasn't the case.

"What's up babygirl?"

"I don't know you, and I do not talk to strangers, so by." I walked passed him and I saw him leave the stoop.

"Wait, wait." He grabs my arm. "We see each other every time you pass through here, so I can't be too strange."

I move his hand from my arm and kept walking, not acknowledging his statement.

"Well, how old are you?" He started walking behind me.

"Too young for you."

"Can't be that young. Not the way you be throwing that thang in them tight ass clothes you be wearing, knowing I be watching it."

He feels on my butt.

"Stop it!" I knock his hand off of me. I picked up my pace.

"Why? You know you want something in between them thick thighs, and I got exactly what you need."

"Leave me alone."

He snatches my hand. "Where you going?"

I push him and take off running towards the other end of the alley. I hear him whistle, and before I could make it to the street, his two friends come from around the corner. I stop in my tracks trying to catch my breath and try to figure what I was going to do next. I turn around and there was Jarell.

"You ain't getting away now."

They drag me into this abandoned building kicking and screaming. Jarell puts his hand over my mouth to stop me from making any noise. They rip off all of my clothes and throw them to the floor.

"Please don't do this." I begged with tears coming from my eyes.

"Bitch I don't care if you beg, I'm still about to get in this pussy." Jarell said with me pinned down by him to an old dirty mattress.

"I bet that pussy tight as hell." His friend Devin says.

"Hell yeah." Jarell co-signs.

The three of them took turns with me, stealing away my innocence. I couldn't fight back. All I could do was cry from the excruciating pain. Why would anyone want to hurt a child like this?

When they were done with me, they run out the building leaving me there. I put on my clothes and walk home. My shirt was torn and dirty, I only had one shoe, and my hair was a mess.

As I walk into the house my mom was coming out of her room.

"Hey Brookie." As she got closer she could tell something was totally wrong. "Baby, what happened? What happened to you? Who did this to you?" She wrapped her arms around me.

"They raped me. They raped me," I cried out.

Everything after that was a blur.

Opening my eyes, I realized I was still in the hospital. My mother, brother and sister where sitting around me.

"Mama." I say, my voice kind of raspy.

"Yes baby."

"Who did this Brook?" Sydney asked. He looked mad. Ever since our dad left, Sydney spent a lot of time in the streets hanging with his friends. Although Sydney was younger than me, he looked out for me like he was the eldest child.

"Jarell and his friends."

Sydney got up and walked out of the hospital room. I knew he was about to go and do something stupid. Probably have one of those older guys that he be around do something to Jarell and his friends or do it himself.

My mom tried to stop him, but it was no use. Sydney took our dad leaving very hard and turned to the streets to raise him.

After a few hours, they released me to go back home. I lay awake in my bed and cried all night long. My feelings were affecting my sister emotionally, because she often took on the emotions of others. She had been suffered from depression and anxiety for a while now. I always tried my best to not let her see me down, but this time I couldn't

Later the next day, Jarell and his friends were arrested, but Sydney and his crew had got to them before the police could.

By the time I returned to school the next week, the news of me being raped had spread. Walking down the halls, all I got was stares. I said nothing to anyone that day. Lydia tried speaking to me, but I ignored her. Even though it wasn't her fault, I blamed her because she wasn't there for me.

"Brook, wait."

I turned around looked at her, rolled my eyes, and kept walking.

When it was time for me to go home, my mom came to pick me up. Before the week ended I needed to change schools, because the pressure was getting to me. I would hear people whispering about me when I walked down the hallways and in the class and I just couldn't take it anymore.

At my new school it was much better. Although they knew about it, no one brought it up to me. While at the school, I met my friend Jessica. She was the first person to ever come up to me and to actually be a friend of mine.

"Hey I'm Jessica. Of course some of us heard what happened, but don't let what you think people are saying or thinking get to you. If you let them see you sweat, then that means that they have power over you. See me, people say things about me all the time, but I never let it get to me, because I know who I am and what they are saying is untrue. There is no need to fight what they say, because they are still going to believe what they want to believe.

I never judge anyone and you seem like a cool person, so I wouldn't mind being friends with you." This was what she said when she first introduced herself to me.

Ever since that day, me and Jessica remained friends, because she taught me that you shouldn't care about what anyone thinks about you, as long as you know who you are and that you should never judge someone without getting to know them first.

Four years had passed by and me and Jessica became close as ever. We had already graduated High School and blossomed into two beautiful young women.

After graduation, I decided to take a break from school while I decided on what I was going to do with my life. I still stayed at home while I looked for a job in the meantime.

Jessica grew into herself a bit more than I did. She had a mean body, curves for days that all the boys adored and she took full advantage of it. Her physic earned her the nickname Jessica Rabbit.

Jey juggled guys like it was a sport. She had a main boo named Chris that had her set up in an apartment, and she had another guy named Marcus who always gave her a fun time. Though Jessica never worked a day in her life, she always had money, and had the newest gear. I didn't judge her how she got hers, because she was the first to accept me for being me.